"Do you have any idea how hard it is not to touch you?" Ben asked.

Before Daisy could take a breath, he reached out and entwined his fingers in her hair. She tried to swallow, but found her throat had gone suddenly dry.

"I wanted you the minute I saw you," he said. "It's a wonder I've lasted this long."

"What ever happened to getting to know a person through dating?" she asked.

"When we met last night, you didn't strike me as someone who was interested in a conventional date, Daisy—you were interested in only one thing from me." He grinned. "But once you found the baby, it gave me a great opportunity—to convince you to want me instead of just . . . a donation."

"I don't want you for that anymore," she said quickly, starting to move away.

"Daisy," he said, catching her arm and pulling her close, "you've got me whether you want me or not."

WHAT ARE *LOVESWEPT* ROMANCES?

They are stories of true romance and touching emotion. We believe those two very important ingredients are constants in our highly sensual and very believable stories in the LOVESWEPT line. Our goal is to give you, the reader, stories of consistently high quality that may sometimes make you laugh, sometimes make you cry, but are always fresh and creative and contain many delightful surprises within their pages.

Most romance fans read an enormous number of books. Those they truly love, they keep. Others may be traded with friends and soon forgotten. We hope that each LOVESWEPT romance will be a treasure—a "keeper." We will always try to publish

LOVE STORIES YOU'LL NEVER FORGET
BY AUTHORS YOU'LL ALWAYS REMEMBER

The Editors

Loveswept ® 701

A BABY FOR DAISY

FAYRENE PRESTON

BANTAM BOOKS
NEW YORK · TORONTO · LONDON · SYDNEY · AUCKLAND

A BABY FOR DAISY

A Bantam Book / July 1994

If you would be interested in receiving protective vinyl covers for your
Loveswept books, please write to this address for information:

Loveswept
Bantam Books
P.O. Box 985
Hicksville, NY 11802

ISBN 0-553-44416-6

Published simultaneously in the United States and Canada

Bantam Books are published by Bantam Books, a division of Bantam Doubleday Dell Publishing Group, Inc. Its trademark, consisting of the words
"Bantam Books" and the portrayal of a rooster, is Registered in U.S. Patent
and Trademark Office and in other countries. Marca Registrada. Bantam
Books, 1540 Broadway, New York, New York 10036.

PRINTED IN THE UNITED STATES OF AMERICA

OPM   0 9 8 7 6 5 4 3 2 1

ONE

Daisy pondered the white paper napkin she had just spent the past few minutes folding into a fan. As far as paper napkin fans went, it was a good one. Holding it up in front of her, she studied its precise creases with as much objectivity as she could muster for the task, and decided that if she chose to be philosophical, the fan could also be viewed as a metaphor for the way she had been feeling about her life lately. It was almost useless.

Behind her, couples gyrated on the X-S Club dance floor to records played by a deejay as lights bounced from the ceiling to the mirrored floor and back up to the dancers. It was eleven-thirty on a Friday night in the Deep Ellum section of downtown Dallas, and the action had not yet heated up. After midnight the music would get louder, the dancing more frenetic, the lights more vivid. It was a scene she was all too familiar with. Sometimes it seemed that a goodly portion of her adult life had been spent in clubs just like this one.

She glanced at her friend Celeste, who was working behind the bar directly across from her, then leaned forward so that Celeste would be able to hear her. "I've made a decision."

"Oh, yeah? You taking off again?"

"No, no. This isn't about another trip. This is an important decision. I've decided I want a baby."

Celeste, a dark-haired beauty with curves that showed to great advantage in her uniform of jeans and a T-shirt inscribed with the name of the club, barely looked up from slicing oranges.

"Did you hear me? I've decided I want a baby."

Celeste grinned. "I heard. I also heard you last month when you decided you wanted a Pekingese."

Daisy reached over and grabbed an orange slice from the compartmented tray Celeste was filling, and took a bite. "Yeah, I know, but I decided against a dog. I travel too much to be a good pet owner."

Celeste paused, the small knife suspended just above the cutting board. "Right. I understand completely—your life-style wouldn't be good for a pet, but it would be just fine for a baby. Daisy, I strongly suggest you rethink this new decision, maybe go back to the idea of the Pekingese. At least you can board a dog."

Daisy pointed at her with the orange slice, causing the gold bangle bracelets she was wearing to slide up her slender arm. "Have a little more faith."

"Hey, call me crazy, but right off the top of my head and with absolutely no experience in the matter I still think a baby would require more care than a pet."

Daisy shrugged. "What can I say? When you're right, you're right, which is why I'm going to change my life. If you counted up all the hours I've spent in clubs like this one, listening to the latest band, it would amount to a sizable chunk of wasted time."

Celeste dumped a jar of olives into one section of the tray. "Well, excuse *me*. *I* happen to spend a great deal of time here."

"That's different. This is your job, and anyway, you go to school during the day."

Her friend was not swayed by her logic. "How can you say your time has been wasted? You've heard a lot of great music, met a lot of nice people—like *me*—and had a fabulous time in the process."

"Okay, maybe it wasn't all wasted time, but I do *need* a change, and I want a baby. It's time I started giving something to someone, and I have a lot of love to give."

"But a *baby*?"

"Yeah," she said softly. "A baby."

She regarded the fan, then tossed it aside, and as she did she noticed the man sitting at the other end of the bar. She couldn't believe she hadn't noticed him before. There was something extremely arresting about him, an unusual stillness and a self-containment that didn't fit in a place where everyone was moving in some fashion or another.

She turned back to Celeste. "It's time I settled down and led a normal life."

"A normal life is relative, Daisy. I mean, times just aren't normal. There just aren't any more *Leave It to Beaver* or *Ozzie and Harriet* families. There probably never were."

"Caleb has finally found a normal life," she said stubbornly.

"Your cousin has married a woman he loves to distraction, but just because he's married doesn't mean he'll ever live a normal life. Don't forget, I *know* Caleb. I mean, where are they now?" Daisy opened her mouth to answer, but Celeste beat her to the answer. "Traipsing around the world on their honeymoon, using chartered planes, boats, and private railway cars. That's nowhere near normal. Normal is *excursion fares*, if you can scrape together the price, or a car with payments too high for you to really afford. Or a clunker, like the one I drive."

Daisy frowned and reached for another paper napkin. Celeste was right, of course. She and Caleb had never quite captured the essence of being normal. And she missed him like crazy. She'd give anything to have him be in town right now. He had always been the mainstay of her life, the person who made her feel secure enough to lead a nomadic life-style.

His getting married hadn't changed their love for each other, but she had tried to make a concerted effort to give Joy and him time together alone. And she couldn't help but feel a little lost without her best friend.

"A baby would help me have a more normal life," she said, going back to the original subject. "And now that I've decided, I want one as soon as possible."

"Uh-huh. Well, unless you're already at the head of someone's adoption list, you're going to have to wait quite a while."

"I know." The man at the end of the bar wasn't model attractive. She didn't think she could even say he was unconventionally attractive. Had his nose been broken? She wasn't close enough to say for sure. But she could tell that his features were rawboned, almost craggy, and that his hair was the color of a rich coffee brown.

Celeste swirled a stack of napkins and placed them on the bar beside the stack Daisy had depleted.

"And actually, if you're thinking of doing the old-fashioned nine-month route—"

"I am, or at least I want to try."

"Then it's going to take a little longer than nine months, since the last time I looked, there was no significant other in your life, nor, I might add, *insignificant* other."

"So what?" She frowned again at the man. Using the light coming from behind the bar, he was reading *The Wall Street Journal*. She didn't think she'd ever seen anyone read *any* kind of paper in a club. A person talked, laughed, listened to music, drank, and danced, but no one ever *read* in this or any music club she'd ever been in. And that wasn't all that was unusual about him. He was dressed in slacks and a sport coat with an open-necked shirt. She'd wager there wasn't one other man there dressed as he was.

She continued to study him, trying to understand why she even cared what he was reading or wore. And then, just as if he had known all along that she was staring at him, he looked up and met her gaze. And she received the impression of a heated intensity strong enough to strip the varnish from the wooden bar that stretched between them.

"As a matter of fact, you never stick with one man more than a week or two."

The comment brought her attention back to her friend. "How very kind of you to point that out."

"Glad to help." With a sassy grin Celeste strolled off to fill an order for a waiter. Upon returning she said, "Of course, if you do this conception thing right, I suppose you need only a week or so with a man. Even an odd moment here or there has been known to do the trick."

Daisy's lips quirked, and she crossed her long legs, causing the flared skirt of the bare little red dress she wore to slide over her upper thighs. "An odd moment? Really, Celeste, you're going to have to quit being so romantic."

"I'm a realist, so sue me."

"At any rate, you're right . . . *if* I were going to go that route."

Celeste came to a standstill. "What other route is there? Adoption? A man? I think that about covers the bases."

She glanced back down the bar. How strange. The man was doing nothing more than sitting there, reading the paper, in his well-tailored conservative clothes, but she thought she detected a hint of danger about him. No, she had to be imagining it. Despite his cut-out-of-stone features, danger simply didn't fit with his conservative attire and reading material. "I don't need a man. All I need is a vial of his sperm."

Celeste's mouth fell open. "Sperm? You're going to a *sperm* bank?"

Daisy nodded absently, her gaze drifting back to

the man. He was drinking something orange, vodka and orange juice more than likely. "I wouldn't hesitate to adopt if for some reason I can't conceive, and one day I may very well adopt. There are a lot of unwanted babies in the world. But if I'm physically able, I'd like to have the experience of carrying and giving birth to a baby that's part me." She rolled her bare shoulders, easing the inexplicable tension that had appeared there in the last few minutes. "And as for a man—I've come to the conclusion that men simply aren't all they're cracked up to be."

"Really?" Celeste sounded clearly dubious.

"Really. Unfortunately they possess the sperm women need to make a baby—a fact that in my opinion is one of nature's little tricks on women. But there are ways around it."

Celeste's voice rose. "Good golly, Miss Molly, I can't believe this. You're really *serious* about going to a sperm bank."

"If I can find one I like."

Celeste shot an annoyed look at a waiter who was calling an order. Pointing a stern finger at Daisy, she said, "Stay there. I'll be right back." She quickly filled the order and returned. "Okay, I know I may regret asking this, but pray tell *what* qualifications would a sperm bank have to have for you to like it? Be decorated in a certain way? Play blues instead of Muzak? Have *Rolling Stone* in the reception area? Oh, no, wait, I've got it. It would have to be financially solvent, have a handsome appearance, and a BMW parked in the driveway."

"Be nice, Celeste." She took a sip of her sparkling water. "First of all, I'd want to make sure that all potential donors had been carefully screened." Her gaze turned once again toward the end of the bar. "For instance, I would want a nice physical specimen . . . like that man down there. Do you know who he is?"

"Nope." Celeste drained a jar of cherries and dumped them into one of the tray's compartments.

"He looks like he's in good physical shape, doesn't he? Strong. Athletic."

Celeste's lovely face split into a wicked grin. "Yeah—good staying power."

Disconcertingly, heat briefly fluttered in the pit of her stomach. She frowned. "I'm not talking about *sex*, Celeste."

"Pity."

"Sex is highly overrated."

"In exactly whose view? Has there been a survey done that I'm unaware of? And who participated? Tibetan monks?"

"I'm talking *genetics*." She cast another glance toward the end of the bar. "It looks to me as if he gets his athletic build from genetics rather than from spending a lot of time in the gym. That would be good."

"Would it? Personally I like to see a man sweating and straining in a gym, testosterone coming off him in waves. I get real excited over the way some men fill out their gym shorts, don't you?"

Daisy's eyes were trained toward the end of the bar. "What's he drinking? Orange juice and vodka?"

"Straight orange juice." She waved a hand in front of Daisy's eyes. "Are you with me, or are you having some sort of out-of-body experience?"

"Sobriety is another quality I would want. In fact, it would be an imperative for a potential sperm donor."

Celeste studied her nails, her expression wry. "Of course, he could be a reformed alcoholic."

Daisy frowned, momentarily deterred. "Yeah, but that could be good too. It would show strength of character and determination to get rid of a bad habit."

Celeste sighed and shook her head. "Would you like another sparkling water?"

"What? Oh, no, I'm fine. He looks like a corporate type, doesn't he? Maybe a stockbroker or an accountant."

"You can tell that just by looking at him? Daisy, are you tracking on all grooves tonight?"

"He's reading *The Wall Street Journal*. He looks like a yuppie to me. This is a leather-and-jeans place, and he's wearing a sport jacket and slacks."

Celeste went back to her work, muttering, "Maybe he hasn't heard that yuppies vanished with the eighties."

"Yeah, but bankers and accountants don't come down here. I mean, Deep Ellum is the funkiest place in Dallas. It's the heart of the cutting-edge music scene. What's he doing here?"

"Why don't you ask him?"

It was a flip remark, but Daisy seriously considered it. She wasn't shy, and she was curious about him. "You know, that's not a bad idea." She slipped off the stool and made her way down to the end of the bar, the skirt of her dress swaying against her legs. "Hi."

He turned toward her, and she received the full impact of light gray eyes, *steel*-gray eyes—the substance rather than the color.

The steel didn't go with the conventional, conservative picture she had painted of him in her mind, and it surprised her. And she could see now that his nose had definitely been broken at least once in his life. It added an interesting toughness to his features.

"Hello."

She nodded toward the paper. "Am I disturbing you?"

His gaze swept over her, faintly insolent, then he slowly smiled, a smile that compelled more than charmed.

"I would imagine you'd disturb most men."

His lips caught her attention. They were full, well formed, and added sensuality to his craggy features. Interesting . . . She extended her hand. "My name is Daisy."

"Daisy," he repeated, taking her hand in his. "Like the flower?"

"Yes, like the flower." She frowned slightly, as she always did whenever anything happened to make her think of her mother. Her name had been a whimsy of her mother's, a spur-of-the-moment decision—like most things had been in her mother's life. "My mother was into her hippy-dippy peace-and-love period."

"There were other periods?"

"Too many to count."

"I think she chose well." He swept a hand over the barstool between them. "Join me."

She moved slightly, then realized she had been about to take him up on his invitation. "No thanks. I was just wondering . . ."

"Wondering what?"

The club was smoke-filled, but she knew she couldn't attribute to the condition of the air the current-seared feeling of her lungs. In search of relief she took a deep breath. "I was wondering if you have ever donated to a sperm bank, and if you have, would you mind telling me which one."

He studied her for a moment, speculation and something else in his gray eyes. "That's quite a line," he said finally. "Do you have a good success rate with it?"

"It's not a line. It's a legitimate question, although I'll be the first to admit that it's a peculiar one."

"Peculiar? You don't do it justice. And by the way, it's a damned shame it's not a line, because it's probably the most original one I've ever heard."

And no doubt he had heard more than his fair share of lines. "It's a question. Do you have an answer to it?"

"The answer is no. I've never donated *anything* to a sperm bank." He paused. "Call me old-fashioned, but I just can't get worked up over a test tube."

Something in the glint of his eye told her she should stop the conversation where it was and walk away. The problem was, she didn't want to walk away, at least not just yet. "I hear it's not that big a deal for a man. *Playboy* might work pretty well."

Never once taking his eyes from her, he folded his paper and carefully, as if it were fragile, set it aside. "Not for me, honey. But *you*, you would work well for me. You *definitely* would work for me."

She stared at him, realizing that she couldn't blame him one bit for his response. She had left herself wide open with her question. She had also well and truly taken leave of her senses. What on earth was she doing talking to a stranger about sperm banks, and *this* stranger in particular, with his conservative clothes and hint of danger about him. "I'm sorry I bothered you." She turned to leave.

His hand shot out and grasped her arm. "Wait a minute. Maybe it's just me, but I thought our discussion was getting pretty damned interesting."

"We weren't having a discussion. I was simply trying to get an answer to a question, that's all."

He grinned, and for an instant she received the distinct and somewhat uncomfortable impression he could see through her to something she couldn't.

"Oh, come on, Daisy. Either we were having a discussion or you were coming on to me—which one is it?"

Through the throb of the dance music his voice came to her with a husky sensuality. "Given the two choices, we were having a discussion."

He nodded. "Right. We were talking about donating sperm and the positive uses of *Playboy*, and you have my total attention. I'm perfectly willing to discuss either subject or go on to another if you like."

She could make a comment or two about total attention, she thought wryly. She was way too interested in him and this conversation. She gazed pointedly at his hand on her arm until he released her, then said, "Look, I shouldn't have asked. It was an impulse, a really *bad* impulse. But I understand quite a few men donate to sperm banks—they'd have to, wouldn't they, to keep them running—and I just thought that if you had, I'd like to know which one."

He eyed her steadily. "Why? Do you think I look like good father material?"

"I don't want you to be a father, just a donor."

"Right. A test tube. How could I have forgotten?"

He hadn't forgotten a thing, she thought, noting the humor in the quirk of his lips. "You know, it's really not that big a thing."

"I'd say that depends on exactly what you're talking about."

She was digging herself in deeper and deeper, she thought, fascinated in spite of herself. As a rule, men offered her no challenge. "I'm talking about donating to a sperm bank."

"Maybe it's not that big a deal to you. You're not the one who would have to have a close intimate relationship with a sterilized glass vial."

She almost smiled. "Point taken."

"Tell me, what do you have against sex?"

She gave a light shrug. "Too many complications."

"But under the right circumstances and with the right person, a helluva lot of fun."

He would be a wonderful lover. The thought came to her from nowhere and without foundation. She crossed her arms beneath her breasts, extremely conscious of being on the defensive. But still, she wasn't willing to leave.

His eyes narrowed. "Why me, Daisy?"

"I obviously don't know you or anything about you. I was just going by appearances, that's all."

"Then you like the way I look."

She was used to playing man/woman games. In fact, she considered herself something of an expert. But for some reason this man, with his calm countenance and compelling grin, was throwing her. He was probably a lawyer, the way he was leading her through this conversation, and she had certainly dated her share of lawyers. "I liked the way you looked," she conceded, because it was the truth.

His eyebrows shot up. "Liked? As in past tense?"

"As in *from a distance.*" She pointed down the bar to the place where she had been sitting. "Through the haze of the smoke."

Her response drew a grin of appreciation from him. "Nice."

"Thanks. It's about time I scored a point in this conversation."

"You've been scoring points since the first moment I saw you." He held out his hand. "My name is Ben."

For a moment she stared at his hand with the same trepidation and fascination an animal might stare at a trap, but then she took it.

He looked down at her hand, then back up at her mouth. "You know, Daisy, if you'd come with me to the sperm bank, stay with me the whole time, and *help* me, I might consider it."

Her hand dropped abruptly from his. Warmth rose in her cheeks. She was blushing, and she couldn't believe it. She *never* blushed. And to make matters worse, he noticed.

He lifted his hand and lightly brushed his fingertips over one cheek. "In fact, I'd do more than consider it."

"Don't bother going to the effort. I'm not interested."

"But *I* am."

She stepped away from him a fraction of a second too slow for her liking. "Ben, it's been a real experience."

"Ah, come on, Daisy—don't leave. I thought you wanted my sperm. Try negotiating. It just might work."

He was having a really good time at her expense, she thought ruefully, but she had to admit she was having a good time too. "What I was mildly, *fleetingly* interested in was your sperm in a *test tube*," she clarified with zest, "and it was only a passing, totally insane thought."

"But it was a unique thought. You have to say that for it—completely unique."

A reluctant smile graced her lips. "Yeah, that

too." She shook her head. "But it was also a *bad* idea."

"I don't know about that. I for one am positively intrigued."

She chuckled. "Good-bye, Ben." With a casual wave of her hand she headed back down the bar to Celeste, who had been watching with interest.

"Well, did you get yourself a donor?"

"I was right in the first place," she muttered, taking cash out of her purse and handing it to Celeste to pay for her sparkling water. "Get a man involved, and you're in trouble."

Celeste threw an appraising gaze at Ben, but Daisy didn't need to look at him to know that he was still watching her with a narrowed, intense gaze. She could feel it, a tangible energy that played over her skin and infiltrated her mind.

"I don't know, honey. I think he's one man who might be worth the trouble."

"No man is," she said curtly, preparing to leave. "But I'm going to get my baby anyway, without a man. You'll see. Talk to you later, Celeste."

"Make sure it's not too much later. I want to be among the first to hear the big announcement."

"Announcement?" she asked. "Oh, right. You mean about me being pregnant. Sure."

She started toward the exit, unable to believe she had gone even momentarily blank on what only a short time before had been an obsession. But Ben was still very much in her mind.

Just before she reached the door, something made her stop and look back at him. She had known he was still staring at her. She had felt the heat of his gaze lasering to her through the lights, the music, and the people.

What was it about him that made her think there was more to him than met the eye? She had reached several conclusions about him—that he was conservative, but also that he was tough, dangerous, compelling. Which was the real man? He was clearly used to handling a woman in any situation from a bed to a bar. And as she stared at him now, she received yet another impression of him, that of a quiet strength that made him seem like an anchor in a place where everyone else was loose and floating.

Interesting. *Too* interesting.

TWO

Street life in Deep Ellum was always colorful, but it was still about an hour away from hitting its eccentric best. In fact, when Daisy exited X-S from the side entrance, she walked out into a relatively quiet night, which was fine with her. After the noise of the club and the interplay with Ben, she welcomed the peace. But, she admitted to herself, she did feel a certain amount of reluctance at leaving him so quickly and so finally. If she came back the next night, would he be there? She frowned at herself. No, a man was not in her plans.

She was about to step out into the street to cross to the parking lot, when she saw two men running down the sidewalk at top speed in her direction. "What—?" As they charged past, one of the men bumped her, sending her reeling back a step. Regaining her balance, she gazed after them, bemused. Cold determination was etched in every line of their bodies. As she watched, they disappeared around a corner. She certainly didn't envy whoever it was they were after. And, she thought wryly, shaking her head, she did *indeed* need to change her life-style.

Still a bit shaken by her encounter with the two men, she hastily crossed the street, climbed into her car, and inserted the key into the ignition.

A soft whisper very near her froze every muscle in her body. Whipping her head around, instinctively bringing her hand to her heart, she glanced toward the passenger seat.

No, not a whisper. A *gurgle*. A *baby* lay there in an infant carrier.

"Good grief, what are you doing here?"

The baby blinked, stuck his fist in his mouth, and began energetically sucking.

Her heart gave a hard thud against her rib cage. She threw a quick glance to the backseat and around the empty parking lot. She saw nothing or no one that would explain what a baby was doing in her car. Damn. Caleb had promised to do something dire to her if she forgot one more time to lock her doors. Oh, well, what he didn't know. . . .

She looked down at the baby. "What the heck—right? Caleb's out of the country." The baby returned her gaze solemnly, sucking and cooing. "I know I said I wanted a baby soon, but this is ridiculous." Her heart melted. A *baby*. Something she profoundly wanted in her life.

She craned her neck and again scanned the parking lot, this time taking more time with her search. She *still* didn't see anyone. "Did someone put you in my car by mistake?" she asked, perturbed, trying hard to make sense out of something that made no sense.

The baby's arms flapped in an uncoordinated motion, then the fist found its way back to the mouth.

"Jeez Louise," she murmured. Thinking she might find some sort of explanation or identity, she tentatively ran her hand between the baby's tiny body and the carrier. She found nothing. The baby was wearing a disposable diaper and a shirt. "Something tells me you're a boy." A quick check told her she was right. A blue blanket covered him. She couldn't be sure of his age, but she guessed between three and four months.

The baby cooed and blew a tiny bubble. Automatically she lifted the edge of the lightweight blanket and wiped his mouth. "Who are you, little one?" she murmured. "And where did you come from?"

The baby cooed again. She smiled at the sweet sound and couldn't resist running her hand gently over his soft head. "You're a real charmer, do you know that?"

Then she noticed the diaper bag resting on the passenger side of the floorboard and went cold. She couldn't stand to think that someone had abandoned him, but what other explanation could there be? And as much as she'd have liked to, she couldn't let herself believe that an angel had heard her say she wanted a baby and delivered one to her. Angels had been nonexistent in her life up until then, and even when she had been a child she hadn't believed the old stork myth.

But there had to be some sort of explanation. There just had to be.

As she got out of the car she scanned the street. She saw people here and there, but no one looked as if they had parked a baby in her car by mistake, nor did anyone look as if they were frantically searching for one. "This is *bizarre*."

She closed the door and went around to the other side and the baby. She leaned in and reached for the glove box and the bottle of aspirin there with its stopper of cotton. Carefully she put a little bit in each of his ears. "Come on, sweetie," she said softly, lifting him and the baby carrier out, then snagged the diaper bag with her spare hand. "We're going to go see if we can find your mommy or daddy, and if we do, I don't want you to watch because it's not going to be pretty. Okay? And *that's* after I give them a piece of my mind."

The baby cooed, and she couldn't resist pressing a kiss to his head. No one but an uncaring monster would go off and leave a baby in an unfamiliar car, and they had better damn well have a good explanation for it. But even as the thought occurred, she knew there could be *no* explanation for abandoning such a precious baby, even if it was meant to be for only a few minutes.

As an afterthought, she locked the car.

Entering the club, Daisy was immediately assaulted by the noise and smoke. Since she spent a lot of time in clubs, she was inured to the atmosphere and conditions. But with the baby in her arms she was now very conscious of the effect of both the noise and the smoke on him.

She looked down at him. He had stilled, and his eyes were wide open, owllike. She brought the carrier up so that she could press her cheek against his. "It's all right, sweetheart," she murmured. "What you're hearing is rock and roll. I know it's hard to believe now, but you're going to love it when you get older."

She made her way through the clusters of crowds

and propped the carrier with its tiny passenger on the bar.

Celeste materialized before her and did a double take. "Wow, that was fast. What did you find? A place that sells instant babies? By the way, I'm sorry, but we don't serve minors."

"Don't give me any trouble, Celeste."

"Trouble? I'm in *awe*." She gazed at the baby with interest. "But shouldn't you at least have given yourself time to set up a nursery or something? Or did this one come complete, no assembly or batteries required?"

"Very funny. Look, here's the deal." She had to speak louder than before since the level of the music had risen since she'd been gone. "I found him in my car. Did you happen to notice any stray parents in here tonight?"

Celeste stared at her. "You're kidding, right?"

Daisy blew out a long breath, as confounded by the situation as her friend. The baby's face was crinkling up in displeasure, and his little body was tensing. Not knowing what else to do, she gently patted him. "Hang in here with me, honey. I promise we won't stay long."

"I'll say this about you, Daisy," a deep, husky masculine voice drawled behind her. "When you say you want something, you don't let any grass grow under your feet."

She whirled to see Ben, his gray eyes full of

amusement. For some reason, the sight of him comforted her. "Do you know who this baby belongs to?"

He raised his hands in a gesture of innocence. "I didn't do it, but out of curiosity, who'd you find? I told you I would be willing under the right circumstances."

"You did?" Celeste asked.

"*Ben!*"

"What right circumstances?"

He threw a careless grin at Celeste. "That she be involved in the process from beginning to end."

Celeste's mouth formed an *O* of fascination as she looked back at Daisy. "And you turned him *down*?"

Ignoring Celeste, she concentrated on Ben.

"No," he said to her, "I don't know who the baby belongs to. Should I?"

"I was hoping someone would. I found him in the car."

Chewing on her bottom lip, Daisy scanned the dance floor. The baby was receiving a few mildly curious looks, but no one seemed truly interested or concerned.

Celeste reached beneath the bar and brought up a phone. "I'll call the authorities. They'll come get him."

A deeply buried instinct Daisy hadn't even been aware she still possessed kicked into action. "*No!*"

She reached out, took the receiver out of Celeste's hand, and slammed it back into the cradle. "I'm not turning this baby over to *any* authority."

Celeste started, clearly disconcerted. "Daisy, if the baby has been abandoned, you need to contact the Children Protective Services. They'll see that he's taken care of."

"You mean they'll put him with a stranger who doesn't know or care about him."

"And you *do*? Daisy, you just found him. I hate to point this out, but you're not making too much sense." Down the bar a waiter called an order. She nodded to him and held up one finger, indicating she needed a minute.

"I don't need to contact anyone. I found this baby in *my* car, I'm perfectly capable of taking care of him, and possession is nine-tenths of the law."

"You can't be serious!" Celeste said, concern now threading her voice. "You can't *honestly* be thinking about keeping the baby."

Daisy glanced at Ben and saw that he was looking at her thoughtfully. She'd been right about him being a great physical specimen, she reflected absently. He was six feet of solid muscles with not an ounce of fat. Lord, why was he on her mind at a time like this?

She put a hand to her head. "I don't know what I'm thinking right now, Celeste, but I do know that until I can find some answers, this baby is my responsibility."

"But it's the law, isn't it? I mean, won't you get into trouble if you don't call someone? Daisy, you could be charged with *kidnapping*."

Celeste was probably right, she thought, once more scanning the club for a clue as to who had left the baby in her car, not troubled a whit about the possible charge. Right now she didn't care what the law was. She knew only that she had a deep, abiding need to make sure the baby was loved and cared for until she could find out who his legal guardian was and why he had been abandoned. And no one could do that better than she could. What she didn't know about babies—which was a lot—she could learn. "I have to go. I have to get him out of here before he loses his hearing and develops lung cancer."

"No, Daisy, wait!"

She picked up the baby and diaper bag. "I can't wait. I'll see you later, Celeste."

"*Daisy!*"

Ignoring Celeste's exhortation, she paused and looked at Ben. He was still watching her, the same thoughtful expression on his face. She couldn't imagine what he was thinking, and as much as she might have liked to know, she simply didn't have the time to find out.

She spared one last moment for her friend, and

smiled reassuringly. "Don't worry. I know what I'm doing."

In fact, she didn't have a clue as to what she was doing, she reflected ruefully, heading back out of the club. She knew only that she couldn't and wouldn't willingly put this baby into the great black sucking hole of the legal system.

She had been there herself as a child, and if it hadn't been for Caleb, she would have been destroyed. She had had Caleb; the baby was going to have her.

Ben stared after her, aware that he wasn't the only man whose gaze followed her. She was the kind of woman a man would instinctively look at, always, even on his last day on earth.

She had sparkling emerald eyes, skin the color of cream, mile-long legs, and red hair that seemed sun-filled even in the muted light of the club. It cascaded over her shoulders in lazy, careless waves and even lazier curls. And her red dress—practically the only spot of color in a place where most everyone wore black—was made up of tiny straps that crossed her back and an outrageously flirty skirt.

She was the kind of woman that once seen, a man would have erotic, lustful dreams about, even if another woman lay by his side. She was the kind of woman about whom a man would have nightmares, trying to figure out how to win even a smile from her.

And her name was Daisy. A smile curved his lips.

She was quite something to behold in her barely-there red dress, carrying a baby with the same look of determination a lioness would have who was bent on protecting her cub.

A foot away from him he heard Celeste give an exclamation and mutter to herself. "Damn! She didn't listen to a thing I said."

"Don't worry," he said. "It was never my intention to let her get away."

The street life had picked up, Daisy noted as she stepped outside into the warm night air. But she wouldn't trust a baby with any of the people she saw. They were club crawlers, the young people and adults who came out at night and danced until dawn. She had once been exactly like them, chasing after good music and fun from club to club, city to city.

Oh, sure, her life was made up of more than travel and clubs. When she was in town, she volunteered at one of the local hospitals. She also helped her friends decorate their homes, as she had Caleb. She had even spent a few months working with

Meals on Wheels, definitely a worthy cause. Knowing that she had been blessed financially, she'd tried to be conscientious in giving to others over the years.

But now she needed something for herself—like the baby in her arms. And she planned on keeping him until she was presented with a good enough reason to give him up.

She started to cross the width of the sidewalk to reach the street, when she suddenly stilled. In the parking lot she saw the beams of two flashlights being directed into first one car and then another. There were two men, moving quickly, searching each car. The memory of the two men who had charged by her earlier in the evening flashed into her head. They were the *same* two men. And they were searching *every* car.

Instinctively she moved back into the deeply recessed doorway and hugged the near wall.

The *baby*. They wanted the baby.

It made sense to her—what else could they be looking for? On the other hand, she was also aware that the theory was pure conjecture on her part. Still something told her she should seriously consider the possibility they were searching for the baby. And *if* they were, it meant they had no idea which car the baby had been left in, so it stood to reason that *they* hadn't been the ones who left the baby in the first place.

As she stood there, debating what she should do, she heard one man call out to the other. Carefully she peered around the edge of the doorway and saw that both flashlights had converged on her car. She tensed. It looked as if they had found something on the ground beside the passenger door.

What could it be. A rattle maybe? A pacifier? Whatever it was, she must have dropped it from the carrier when she had lifted the baby from the car.

She glanced down at him. In the relatively clean air and with the noise from the club muted, he had quieted. His little eyes had grown heavy and were just about to droop closed. He was so innocent, so helpless. *No one* was going to get their hands on this baby until she knew for certain they were entitled to him and meant no harm.

The sound of glass breaking startled her out of her reverie. They had smashed her car window, and she was sure now that they were after the baby. The rattle, or whatever it was, had linked her car to the baby.

The club door opened behind her. "What's going on?" Ben asked quietly.

She glanced around at him. "There are two men over there in the parking lot, searching for something, and they just broke into my car. Damn, I knew there was a reason I never locked my car."

"Come back into the club. I'll call the police."

"No. They're looking for the baby."

"Are you sure?"

"Pretty sure. I must have dropped something of the baby's on the ground, and they found it."

"What if one of them is the baby's father?"

"Then he's not very careful with his baby."

"Maybe not, but legally and until a court says differently, he would have a right to his child."

She shook her head, rejecting what he had just said. "I saw those two when I left the club the first time. They were chasing someone, and I'd stake everything I own that they're up to no good. I'm simply not willing to turn the baby over to them until I know more."

"Then what do you plan to do?" His voice was calm, as if he didn't think it at all strange to find her lurking in a doorway with a baby who wasn't hers, hiding from two men she didn't know.

"I guess I need to wait here until they leave and hope they don't think about coming over."

"That's no good. When they don't find what they're searching for in your car, they're going to look for you."

"You mean the baby."

"Daisy, *you* have the baby. And they're going to be able to identify you by your car."

She gazed up at him, wondering what she was going to do and wondering why he was there with her, talking to her as if he had a stake in the matter.

"I'll call a cab and have it come to an address a couple of doors down from the club."

"Too obvious and too risky. Wait here. I have a nice, nondescript rental car. I'll get it."

She shook her head again. "They'll see me in the streetlights."

"No they won't, not if you're quick enough."

He pulled out a handkerchief from his pocket, reached up into the cage of wire that surrounded a light bulb, and unscrewed it. Darkness instantly cloaked them. "Stay here and watch for me. I'll pull up at the curb."

With her heart pounding, she tightened her grip on the baby's carrier, bringing him closer against her. It looked as if the men were giving her car a thorough search, but that wouldn't take them too long. And then what?

Time seemed to crawl, but a minute couldn't have passed before a light tan car rolled to a quiet stop directly in front of her, the passenger side facing her, and the door swung open.

She slipped out of the shadowed doorway and into the car, and then the car was moving, down a narrow, side road that was less-traveled than the street in front of the club. In another few blocks he took a right, then a left.

She was beginning to breathe a little easier. "Your headlights aren't on."

"Yeah, I know." He glanced in the rearview

mirror, took another turn, then flicked the headlights on.

She glanced around her, confused. She had lived
a number of years in Dallas, but after only a few
minutes he had her feeling lost. As near as she
could figure out, they appeared to be in a residen-
tial district, heading away from downtown Dallas.
"Where are we?"

"We're not where those two guys are."

That was certainly true enough, she thought.
Then she saw a small light bulb lying in the opened
ashtray. She glanced over her shoulder and up. *The
dome light*. It hadn't come on when she had gotten
into the car.

He glanced at her. "I took it out so they wouldn't
see you."

"Clever," she said faintly, her gaze returning to
the light bulb in the ashtray. It was something she
would never have thought of doing. But he had. It
was then she realized that she had gotten into his
car without a thought as to the consequences.

"Where to?" he asked.

Good question. Her first impulse was to have
him take her home, but . . .

He spoke before she could. "You know that they
will have found your registration, don't you? And if
not that, your car insurance. Both documents will
have your home address on it."

"I was just thinking the same thing." She tossed

alternate plans around in her head. Where could she go? Caleb was out of the country, so she couldn't go to him for help. She had the key to his house, but it was right next door to hers. If those men were serious about finding the baby—and she didn't have any reason to think otherwise—she didn't want the baby anywhere near when they came looking.

Serious doubts began to creep into her mind. She was sitting in the car of a man she had met only that night, with a baby that wasn't hers. In short, she was in one hell of a mess.

She slanted a sideways glance at Ben. The truth was, she knew nothing at all about him except that he reacted with extreme cool in an emergency. Perhaps that was good. After all, it very much appeared that she was smack in the middle of one extra-large emergency.

On the other hand . . .

THREE

It hadn't even occurred to her not to go with Ben.

Daisy stared at the small light bulb in the ashtray and contemplated what she had just done. She'd been in a situation she had needed to get out of immediately, and without thought she'd gone with him. So, okay—she and the baby were safe, at least for the time being, and she had given herself some breathing space. So far so good.

Now she had to decide what she was going to do. She had about fifty dollars with her, but her ATM card was at home in another purse. She did have a credit card though. . . .

"Have you decided where you want to go?"

"To a hotel, one on the outskirts of downtown.

It'll give me a chance to think about all of this and decide the best course of action."

Ben shook his head. "If you're planning on charging the room with a credit card, don't. It's fairly easy for someone to trace you through electronic methods. All they need is a laptop computer and a phone jack."

Her forehead wrinkled with consternation. "How do you know that?"

He shrugged. "It's common knowledge."

"Oh, yeah? To whom?" He didn't answer, and the baby stirred in his carrier, whimpering. His eyes, though, remained closed. She patted him, trying to reassure him. She sympathized wholeheartedly with the little guy. If he was a stranger to her, she was most definitely a stranger to him. He must be wondering where his mother was, a question she herself would dearly love the answer to.

Surreptitiously she glanced at Ben. The streetlights they passed played in shifting patterns over his face, at times making him appear almost menacing. But she had no reason to think he was. He was grasping the steering wheel with hands that were clearly strong and competent, though when he had grasped her arm in the club, his touch had been very gentle. And disturbing . . .

He had said his car was a nondescript rental, and it certainly was. It was a standard four-door with no frills. Whenever she had occasion to rent a car, she went for the top of the line. So what did the car tell her about him? Nothing new really. In fact, the car fit her original impression of him, that he was conservative and traditional. But without knowing why, she'd also perceived an element of danger in him. She had to be wrong. Simply because a man thought fast and took control didn't mean he was a threat.

"Well, Daisy?" His patient voice cut through her turbulent thoughts.

"I suppose I could spend the night at a friend's, but since at this point I don't really know what I've gotten myself into, I'd rather not bring anyone else into it right now."

"That's smart. Until you know *if* you're in danger, what it is, and how much it is, I would suggest isolating yourself."

"I agree." She hesitated. "And that includes from you." He slanted a steel-hard gaze to her, but she went on. "You've been great, and I probably couldn't have gotten away from X-S so smoothly without your help, but it's time we parted company."

"You think so, huh?"

"Yes, I do." The baby's fretting was increasing and his eyes were opening. She shifted him in his carrier in an attempt to make him more comfortable. "Look, there's no need for you to put yourself at any more risk. Just take me to a hotel. Those men aren't going to be able to trace one night's receipts that quickly, and if I decide it's necessary, I can move to another place tomorrow." And first thing, she thought, she'd hire a detective.

"Whether or not they're going to be able to trace the receipt with any speed depends on how resourceful they are. It also depends on the hotel and how quickly the management calls your credit card in. Most hotels do it as soon as possible so that they can make sure your credit is good and that they're not going to get stuck with a nonpaying guest."

"Still . . ."

"And as for moving to another place tomorrow—how? Are you going to rent a car? How? How much cash do you have? You've got to eat. How? It may take you several days to figure out what's going on, and that will add up to quite a few meals. You may be thinking about hiring a detective. By what means? Do you have enough money to buy yourself food, plus whatever the baby needs, plus pay for cabs or a rental car?" His gaze trailed down her body, taking in the way the bare red dress clung to her curves. "I would think," he said, a new huskiness entering his voice, "that a change of clothes would also be a good idea, and that's going to take more money. Where are you going to get it?"

His words unnerved her almost as much as his inspection of her. "*How* do you know to ask those questions?" There was more than a little suspicion in her voice. "Sooner or later I would have probably thought of them—one at a time—but you thought of all of them instantly."

He shrugged. "It's just common sense."

She smoothed her hand over the baby's head. His fussiness was getting worse and her nerves were sharpening. She wished she had more experience with a baby. She wished she knew what to do about her predicament. She wished she weren't so attracted to Ben. "Well, common sense or not, *none* of those things is your problem."

"Maybe you're right, but you're going to have to face each and every question, and I can help."

"Thanks, but you've done enough. I'll manage."

"I'm sure you will, but you'll manage better with my help." He made another turn, this time onto a main street. "We'll go to my hotel. You can stay with me."

Her head swung around to him, sending her hair sliding over her shoulders. "No."

With his eyes steadily on the road, he sighed. "Okay, Daisy . . . think for a minute. What was in your car?"

Her brows drew together. "What do you mean?"

"When's the last time you cleaned it out. Could there have been a carbon of a deposit slip for instance? A credit card receipt? An address book?"

She groaned and rubbed her forehead. "Oh, Lord. There could be all that and more."

"You have to consider something, Daisy," he said, speaking very slowly, as if he were giving great thought to each word. "Assuming those were bad guys back there—"

"They weren't good guys."

"—and by taking the baby and running—"

"It was the only thing I could think to do."

"Fine, but by doing that you've just cut yourself off from any security backups you might normally have. There's nothing or no one familiar you can turn to without the fear of being traced and caught."

His words shocked her.

"But if you turn to a stranger, namely me, you'll have a chance. Face it. My hotel is the only answer. There's nothing to trace you to me."

"Celeste—"

"Do you think she'll say anything if she's questioned?"

She thought of Celeste's no-nonsense personality. "No. She's likely to take their heads off for asking."

The baby gave an angry cry, and her anxiety mounted. What should she do? She had to decide the *best* thing to do for this tiny person. Second best wouldn't do.

She lifted him from the carrier to her shoulder

and gently patted his back. "Shhh. It's going to be all right, it is." Lord, she *hoped* it would be. Apparently the baby also had doubts, because his crying grew louder.

Ben turned onto yet another side street, and to her surprise pulled into a dark driveway and switched off the car. "Where are we? What are you doing?"

Calmly he reached into the backseat for the diaper bag. "I know you don't trust me, Daisy, and there's really no reason why you should." He opened the bag and peered in. "Great, there's a can of formula in here and a couple of bottles. I was hoping there would be. At least now we'll know what to feed him."

Damn. Daisy silently chastised herself. She should have thought to look in the diaper bag.

His gaze returned to her. "Anyway, whether you want to admit it or not, I'm your best shot."

"But how can I know that for sure?"

"You can't. You're just going to have to trust me." He reached down and flicked a lever on the side of his seat, sending the bench seat backward, increasing the room between him and the steering wheel. Twisting around, he lifted the crying baby from her arms and lay him down between them.

The baby instantly quieted, as if his new handler and position interested him. He stared solemnly up at Ben, and she received the funny feeling that he knew someone knowledgeable had taken over.

"Trust you?" she asked, her voice more strident than she would have wished because she was still irritated that she hadn't immediately known what to do for the baby. "You just said there was no reason I should trust you."

He glanced at her. "Yeah, but it looks very much as if you're going to have to find a reason, doesn't it?"

She let out a long breath. How could her life have changed so dramatically in such a short time? And all because of one tiny baby. Still, she couldn't be more committed to him if he were her own flesh and blood. A child needed someone he could depend on, and for the time being she seemed to be that person for this little one.

"Here's the situation you're in, Daisy. If you're completely serious about protecting this baby, then you're going to have to figure out a safe place to stay where no one can find you and somehow pay for that place along with food. I'm your answer. I already have a place. I can pay for both it and anything else you might need."

"But *why*? Why would you even want to? Why would you consider saddling yourself with a woman and a baby on the run?"

He whipped out a fresh diaper and with quick,

efficient movements set about changing the baby. "You don't know?"

"How would I know?"

He flashed a grin that slipped beneath her skin, an inexplicable irritant, as if he were rubbing velvet the wrong way and she could somehow feel it.

"It's very simple, Daisy. I feel responsible."

"Why?" she asked again, having a hard time following his line of thought.

His grin widened. "Why not? After all, we were going to make a baby together, and this will be like a trial run."

Staring at him, she fought to keep her voice at a normal level when she spoke. "We were going to do no such thing."

"No?" Apparently unperturbed by her answer and through with the diapering, he turned back to the diaper bag and searched through it until he found a cloth pad.

"*No.*"

"You know what? That's really strange." He placed the cloth on her right shoulder and smoothed it down over the curve of her breast with a deft, maddeningly impersonal hand. He even grazed her nipple with the heel of his hand. Her breath caught in her throat and uncharacteristic warmth flooded through her. She looked hard at him, searching for something that would tell her he knew exactly the effect he had had on her, but his face was absolutely expressionless.

She knew she was going to regret asking her next question, and with a sigh she got it over with. "Why is it strange?"

"Because I received the definite impression from our conversation in the club that we were going to make a baby together."

"Not *together*."

"I don't know about that. You showed a *very* specific interest in my sperm, Daisy, and to my mind it's pretty much the same thing. In fact, it's *exactly* the same thing."

She dropped her head in her hand. "Could you please just forget that conversation?"

His lips twitched as he picked up the baby and carefully handed him back to her. "Forget the all-time best conversation I've ever had with a woman? Now, that would be hard to do."

The baby was crying again, and she was torn between giving Ben a searing retort and trying to find something to make the baby stop crying. She tried jiggling him and talking softly.

After watching her for a minute, Ben reached over and positioned the baby so that he was cradled in her arms against her. As he did so, his hand once again touched her breast lightly, as if by accident, but this time with enough purpose for her to question whether it had really been an accident or not.

Whatever his intent, her skin burned as if she had gotten too close to a fire and her nipples hardened as if he had taken them into his mouth.

Before she could say anything, Ben produced a bottle from the diaper bag and handed it to her. "It's not warmed, but it's not cold either and the temperature shouldn't upset his stomach. At this point he just wants food."

Sure enough, the baby latched hungrily onto the nipple and began sucking with gusto.

"Now, there's a little guy who knows what's important," Ben said softly, gazing down at the baby.

What she saw in his expression made her instantly rethink her situation. Compassion was there in his gaze, as well as an aching tenderness. He wouldn't hurt the baby—she understood that now with bone-deep certainty. And she could take care of herself.

Couldn't she?

The hotel Ben was staying at turned out to be conservative and moderately priced. He was in a businessman's suite that consisted of a small living and kitchen area off the bedroom. Nothing lavish, but certainly adequate and comfortable.

"You and the baby can take the bedroom. I'll sleep out here." With a wave of his hand he indicated the sofa. "It pulls out into a bed."

Daisy stood in the middle of the room with the baby cradled in her arms and eyed the couch doubtfully. "Are you sure you'll be comfortable on it? The mattress is probably not that great."

Something flickered in the depths of his gray eyes, a mischievousness underscored with a resolute seriousness. "I'm open to another suggestion if you are."

Her impulse was to rise to the bait, but from her limited experience with him she knew she wouldn't get very far. She'd be much better off ignoring the suggestive nuances of his words. "The baby and I can take the couch. There's no point in you being uncomfortable because of my problems."

His lips curved slowly into a smile. "Don't worry about it. With you in the general vicinity, I have a feeling I'll be uncomfortable whichever bed I sleep in tonight."

"Ben—"

"Sorry, but it's true. However, it's one of those things we'd be better off talking about later. For now, let's see if we can fix a safe bed for the baby." Without waiting to see if she would follow, he strolled into the bedroom.

By the time she arrived, he was already moving the covers and the pillows on the king-size bed.

"The baby may or may not be able to roll over,

but if we lay him horizontally against the headboard and surround him by pillows, he should be safe."

She understood immediately. "That's a wonderful idea. And I'll sleep beside him across the end of the bed."

They had stopped at a convenience store on the way to the hotel, and Ben had gone in and stocked up on diapers, waterproof pads, more formula, and an all-important pacifier. It was the pacifier, she had decided, that she must have dropped beside her car.

Ben spread the soft pads over the bottom sheet, then reached for the sleeping baby and laid him on his side amid the pillows. Straightening away, he eyed the space left with a critical eye. "You should have plenty of room."

"I'll be fine." She returned to the living area wearily sank down in one of the two armchairs and waited for Ben. It didn't take long.

"You've got something on your mind?" he asked, dropping onto the couch.

"Don't tell me you're surprised."

He slowly smiled, a smile filled with a combination of gentleness and humor that she found incredibly sexy. Her first impression of him had been that he was more intriguing than attractive, but when he smiled at her, he could actually make her heart pound harder, her toes curl, and her insides heat. And the more time she spent with him, the more attractive he became to her. Oh, yes, the man was definitely dangerous but not for the initial reason she had thought.

"Hey," he said softly, "you can relax now. I know that a lot of things have happened really fast and that you've had to make instant decisions. If it's any comfort, I think you've made the right decisions."

"That's not too surprising," she said wryly, "since several of those decisions concerned you and I did exactly what you said."

Once again he sent her a smile that compelled and affected her. Amazing, she thought. And fascinating. She was used to affecting men. She wasn't used to men affecting her. In some curious way it was as if the balance of nature had been upset and she had been left feeling frayed around the edges.

"Relax, Daisy. You're safe."

To a certain extent she did feel safe or she wouldn't be with him there now, she reflected, watching him as he shrugged out of his sport coat. But she didn't like the way he had of keeping her off balance. More puzzling, she knew he wasn't doing it on purpose.

He neatly folded his jacket and laid it over the back of the couch with care. Even if he didn't hang it up, which she would bet money he soon would, there would be no wrinkles in the jacket in the morning. He relaxed his lean, muscled frame back against the couch. "Okay, Daisy, fire away."

Direct, she thought. The man was definitely direct, at least about some things. "Okay . . . who are you and what are you doing in Dallas?"

A small smile played around his lips. "I've already introduced myself to you."

"Right. You said your name is Ben, but you didn't give me a last name."

"And a last name would make you feel as if you know me better?"

"It would be a start."

"Okay, my full name is Ben McGuire. Well, actually it's Benjamin Elliot McGuire, but I've been Ben for as long as I can remember. Now you tell me your last name."

She was slightly incredulous that they hadn't even known each other's last names. "Huntington. Daisy Huntington."

He nodded solemnly. "How do you do, Daisy Huntington."

She blew out a long stream of air, directing it upward so that it stirred the ends of her hair that fell across her forehead. "I've been better."

"You couldn't prove it by me. I think you're fantastic."

She started. "You do?"

"Absolutely. I can't think of one other woman who's ever gotten my attention as fast as you did, and with just one question."

Her expression darkened. "I've asked you to forget that."

His smile broadened. "Ah, Daisy, you do ask the impossible. The idea of having a baby with you has definitely piqued my interest."

"Not *with* me. That's the part you never seemed to get. Your participation was never meant to be more than purely clinical."

"I've heard it called a lot of things, Daisy, but never clinical."

With a sigh she rubbed her forehead. "How can I make this clear to you? Actually, I'm positive that you do understand. It's just that you won't accept it."

He grinned. "Faced with the choice of a beautiful woman or a test tube, I'll go with the beautiful woman every time. Call me crazy."

It hadn't been a direct compliment, but she was pleased. The conversation definitely wasn't going the way she would have liked it to go. "You know the Tuna Helper you can buy in the grocery store?"

"Tuna Helper?"

"Right. Tuna Helper. When you want a tuna casserole you can go get yourself a box of this stuff, mix it with a can of tuna, and, *voilà*, you have a tuna casserole."

"Who in their right mind would want a tuna casserole? I can't think of too many other things I dislike as much as tuna."

"I wasn't really talking about tuna or a tuna casserole, Ben."

"Funny, I could have sworn you were."

"No, it was only an example. Pay attention."

"I can't think of one other person who has ever had as much of my attention as you do at this moment."

"Good, because I want you to understand this. You mix one thing with another and get something you want. But the point is—"

"I can hardly wait for this."

"The point is you don't have to deal with anyone else to get that Tuna Helper. You see? There's no emotional commitment to the process."

"There probably was for the tuna, since he would have to give up his life so that you could have tuna casserole."

"There was no emotional commitment on *my* part, exactly, as I intend the process to be when I obtain the sperm that's going to help make my baby. I'm going to go to a store and buy it."

"Well, speaking as the Tuna Helper in this little metaphorical analogy, I can categorically say that it would require quite a bit of emotional commitment on my part, not to mention energy."

She crossed her arms in front of her. "Which

is exactly why I'm no longer considering you as a possible donor."

"I'm inconsolable."

"You'll get over it."

His expression changed, became more serious. "Tell me something—do you still want a baby?"

"Of course. Why wouldn't I?"

He nodded toward the door to the bedroom. "I thought maybe taking care of that little fella in there might have given you a dose of reality."

"The reality so far is that you've been doing most of the work. It's true I may not know as much as you do about babies—"

"Do you know anything at all?"

She shrugged. "I've never taken care of a baby before. I've never even done any baby-sitting for anyone. But I'm a real fast learner, and believe me when I say that that baby in there will want for nothing."

"So then you're still okay with your decision about not calling the authorities?"

"Absolutely."

"It's not too late, Daisy."

"Why would you even bring that up?"

"Because you don't know anything about that baby, and taking care of him is going to be a huge responsibility. No one would blame you for handing him over. In fact, it's probably the right thing to do."

"It is positively, absolutely, *not* the right thing to do." Her voice was flat, her expression set. "No child should ever have to get mixed up in the legal system."

He eyed her consideringly. "You're not thinking of keeping the baby for yourself, are you?"

She tried for a nonchalant air and failed. The baby in the next room, whoever he was, had become instantly important to her, probably far more important than was good for her. But she understood all too well how helpless a child could feel when caught up in a situation that was out of the child's control. She hoped the baby's young age would prevent him from being scarred permanently, like her, but she didn't think any expert could say that for sure. A child's psyche was formed at an early age. "If I find out his parents have abandoned him, I will take him in a minute."

"You're remarkable. There aren't many women who would be willing to take on someone else's responsibility."

"The moment he was placed in my car, he became *my* responsibility."

"No, not really."

"Yes, Ben, really. But you, you're another matter. You may know a lot about babies . . . By the way, where *did* you get your experience? Are you one of those traveling salesmen who has a wife and five children back in Topeka?"

"Darn, you've guessed my secret."

She regarded his smile with a frown. "You know, you have a knack of answering my questions without really giving me a concrete answer."

"What do you want to know?"

"Well, for instance, what are you doing in Dallas?"

"I'm here on business."

"What kind?"

"Oh, I'm sort of a jack-of-all-trades."

"Really? What—" A faint sound from the other room made Daisy turn her head around. "Was that the baby?"

"He's just making noises in his sleep."

She jumped up and went to the bedroom door to peer in. Sure enough, the baby was sound asleep and hadn't moved.

She slowly returned to the living area and Ben. She knew his full name now and that he was a self-professed jack-of-all-trades. And somehow and with very little effort he had managed to make the idea of spending the night in his hotel suite acceptable to her. She was torn between wanting to know more about him and keeping a safe emotional distance from him. She clasped her hands together in front of her and adopted a formal tone. "Ben, I'd like to thank you. He's not *your* responsibility, but you've been an enormous help."

His lips twitched. "You're entirely welcome."

Unable to stand there beneath his steady gaze, she wandered toward the small kitchen.

"Are you hungry?" he asked. "It's too late to order room service, but—"

"Too late? What do you mean?"

"I mean the kitchen closes at eleven."

She always stayed in hotels that provided twenty-four-hour room service. "Isn't that inconvenient? Why don't you stay in a better quality hotel?"

"There's nothing wrong with this one. It suits me fine."

"But what do you do when you get hungry in the middle of the night?"

"I'm usually asleep in the middle of the night."

She opened her mouth to comment on how boring his life sounded, but then closed it again. First of all, his life, boring or not, was none of her business. And secondly, she had the sure feeling she would lose in the exchange. Sure enough, even without her saying a thing he fulfilled her expectations.

"I sleep if there's nothing more interesting to do, but since you're here, I'm perfectly willing to stay up as long as you like and engage in any and all activities of your choice."

He didn't look one bit tired, she reflected. What had Celeste said about him? Oh, yes, *staying power*. She had to agree with her friend on that one. She imagined he could make love to a woman all night long and still make an eight A.M. meeting, sharp as a tack. For lack of something better to do, she stepped into the tiny kitchen and opened the refrigerator. "Milk?" She glanced over her shoulder at him. "You actually drink milk?"

"Milk is good for you, didn't your mother ever tell you?"

"No." In fact her mother had never given her any advice that she could remember, and her father had been even less help, exiting her life early.

Warmth spread along her back as Ben walked up behind her, and she realized she'd spent the last minute staring into an almost empty refrigerator.

"Would you like a glass?" His hand reached out and rested on top of the door beside hers.

"No." She straightened and turned, inadvertently brushing against his body. Instinctively she stilled and discovered she was standing within the circle of Ben's open arms, and his body heat was more than counteracting the chill from the refrigerator. "Well," she said, and swallowed, "maybe a little glass."

He lifted his hand and wound a loose wave of her hair around his finger. "If you and I *were* to make a baby together," he said softly, "and he or she looked like you, it would be the most beautiful baby ever born."

Something hard and hot knotted in her stomach. She didn't want to move, didn't want to speak. She waited, waited . . . and was rewarded.

He kissed her lightly at first, as if he were curious and experimenting with the feel of her lips and the flavor of her taste. She could have drawn away at any time, but she chose to stay where she was. She supposed she was curious too. After all, earlier that night he had sufficiently intrigued her so that she had walked down the length of the bar to talk to him. He had kept her at his side longer than she had intended. He had talked her into staying the night with him. And he *still* intrigued her.

The heat of his body increased. She could feel it, wrapping around her, even though his hands weren't touching her. His lips were firm and sure on hers, and his scent was like him, quiet and slightly mysterious with an intriguing hint of spice and musk. Nice, she thought hazily, hardly aware that her mouth was relaxing, her lips parting.

This wasn't a kiss to draw away from. On the contrary, she found herself leaning closer to him, seeking his heat, his scent, his strength. The kiss deepened by minute stages, became hotter by degrees. She wasn't sure when his tongue slipped into her mouth, but her tongue automatically assumed possession, sliding against it, learning its texture. And she wasn't sure when her arms encircled his neck, but it was fine with her that it had happened. She had simply needed to be steadied, to be closer to him, to feel his body against hers.

The kiss went to her head, making it swim, to her body, making it ache, to her heart, making it pound harder. It was a kiss that seemed to go on and on. It was a kiss that ended all too soon.

FOUR

A sound pierced Daisy's thick cloud of sleep. During the night she had been too conscious of the baby next to her to do more than doze in snatches. She wasn't used to the soft little noises an infant made in sleep, and she had spent part of the night simply watching the funny expressions that crossed his face and wondering what his dreams were made of. A couple of times she had thought he was about to wake, but she had gently rubbed his back, soothing him until once again he settled into sleep.

He was a good baby, and she couldn't fathom a reason anyone would abandon him. But then, she knew better than most that the mothering instinct was not inherent in all women.

Toward dawn she must have fallen into a deep

sleep, but now she heard the sound again—the baby was waking up. Even as the realization occurred to her, she became aware of a warm presence very near her. Her eyes slitted open, and she saw Ben leaning over her.

Ben, his chest bare, his expression tender, his eyes soft.

The memory of the kiss they had shared hours before came back to her. She had wanted it to go on and on, but he had ended it. Now he was above her, reaching for her. Still caught and held by drowsiness, still wanting him, she began to raise her arms.

But instead of coming down to her, he reached to the side of her. The baby. He was reaching for the *baby*.

Something was very wrong with this picture.

A man was leaning over her on a bed, but he was reaching for a baby instead of her.

It wasn't as if she'd had that many experiences of a man reaching for her in bed. In fact, there had been very few. But she still found herself wanting to laugh at herself. And *worry*. The fact that even for an instant she had wanted him indicated to her that her mental stability must be slipping. Badly.

She struggled upward. "What are you doing?"

"The baby has been awake for the last few minutes, and he's hungry."

She pushed her hair from her face and gazed

at the tiny human next to her. His eyes were wide open and his arms were frantically waving in the air as he fussed and squirmed. "I didn't hear anything until just a few seconds ago," she said, troubled.

"You were sound asleep. You must have had a rough night."

"It wasn't too bad." A draft of air on her bare thighs caught her attention. She looked down to see that she was wearing one of Ben's shirts, a soft blue cotton that carried his scent. Masculine. Mysterious. Musk and spice.

Tugging the shirttail down as far as it would go, she remembered how he had ended the kiss, and then, as if nothing had happened between them, had calmly offered her one of his shirts to sleep in. But though he had seemed perfectly composed, she had sensed a tension in him. And in her. The kiss *had* happened, both of them had been deeply affected by it, and they both knew it. She scooted toward the edge of the bed.

"Don't get up. I've already changed his diaper—"

His words stopped her where she was on the bed. "You've been in here, watching me sleep?"

His grin was suspiciously mischievous. "No, I was changing the baby's diaper. I also started a bottle warming in the next room."

She grimaced and quickly glanced at her watch. "You're entirely too efficient for this early in the morning. Some people might find that disgusting. Like *me*, for instance."

"Go back to sleep, Daisy. I was just about to take him into the next room and feed him."

"Nope. That's my job." She slid to her feet. "Give me a minute." She retreated to the bathroom and emerged a short time later feeling better with her face washed and her teeth finger-scrubbed with his toothpaste.

Ben was cradling the baby, and she held out her arms for the infant, then carefully brought him against her. He was adorably soft and smelled sweet, like clean, fresh innocence. She pressed a kiss to his head. She'd never known before how infinitely kissable a baby's head could be. "Good morning, sugar pie. How are you doing this morning?"

The baby focused on her and gave a little fretful cry. She kissed him again. "Not much for small talk in the morning? Believe me, I sympathize. And you want breakfast, right?" She smiled down at him. "Well, come with me, young man, right this way. . . ."

In the next room she settled with him on the couch and presented him with the bottle Ben handed to her. The baby immediately quieted.

Ben set a cup of hot coffee on the table next to her. "Do you take anything in your coffee?"

"No, black is great, thanks."

He nodded. "Sure. When you get ready we can order breakfast from room service or go out, whatever you like." He dropped into a chair and began rummaging in the diaper bag.

He was wearing a pair of tailored slacks, she noticed. And since she'd gotten up, he'd slipped on a shirt, but he hadn't gotten around to buttoning it. When he moved, the sides flared out, giving her enticing glimpses of bronze skin, a light covering of brown chest hair, and a muscled abdomen. A night's growth of beard darkened his jaw, and his feet were bare. She was suddenly struck by how intimate their situation was, how full of potential. . . .

He looked over at her and met her eyes, and she felt something tangible spark between them, something basic and sexual. She had to face it. With breathtaking ease and power he could ignite desire in her—desire that formed hard, hot, and deep in her loins, impossible to ignore. She couldn't think of one thing to say to him that wouldn't reveal what she was thinking and feeling.

He was the one who finally broke the silence. Nodding toward the baby, he said, "You're good with him. You have a natural instinct."

"Thanks. I told you I would learn fast."

"So you did."

He gazed at her a moment longer, his eyes

lingering on the length of her legs, and she couldn't help wondering if his thoughts about her were coming close to approximating hers about him. If they were, she might be in a world of trouble. Thankfully he soon returned his attention to the diaper bag, delving through it.

"There's a small box of cereal in here. I presume he's being started on solid foods."

"Solid? Really? Gosh, he's so little."

"Remember, we're not sure exactly how old he is. At any rate, we should at least offer him some and see if he'll take it."

"I guess you're right. I wish he'd come with a set of instructions."

"Don't worry about the baby. He'll let us know what he needs."

She dropped her gaze to the diaper bag in an attempt to sever the charged connection with him. But exactly as if he were holding her in an embrace, she could feel the power of him all around her. That world of trouble she'd been contemplating moments before came crashing down on her. He wanted her, of that she was certain. And there was something else she was certain of too—she didn't want to think of the women he had known and wanted before last night.

"Daisy?"

"What? Oh, I don't know about that. He can't even tell us his name."

"It doesn't seem to me as if he minds you calling him sugar pie."

She sighed and gazed down at the baby, who was concentrating intently on his bottle. "I'm probably scarring him for life in some way."

He grinned. "I doubt it. And trust me, he can tell us when he's hungry or wet or even when he just wants attention."

Us. He had said *us.* She didn't know what was going to happen in the next minute, much less the rest of the day, but she did know that she should probably try to get away from Ben—for her sake. "Not us, Ben, *me.* You've helped us so far, but now it's up to me."

He gazed at her for several moments, his expression shuttered "You, huh? So, okay, what are you going to do?"

"Well . . . I suppose the first thing I should do is check the paper to see if there is any mention of a missing baby."

He nodded. "That makes sense."

Something in his noncommittal tone made her eyes narrow. "You already thought of that, didn't you? In fact, you've probably already looked."

"There's no mention of anything."

She stared at him, as curious about him as ever. "Tell me something—what were you doing in X-S last night?"

"I was reading the paper."

"Right. Of course. How stupid of me."

His features softened. "And I was being hit on by one *very* beautiful redhead with the world's best *ever* pickup line."

She held up a finger. "Don't even think about starting that again."

His lips twitched. "Did anyone ever tell you that you look fairly passable in the morning?"

"Passable? Gee, thanks."

"You're welcome."

She had to fight hard not to tell *him* that he looked like sex personified in the morning. "As soon as I get this little guy here fed and dressed, I'm going to see about hiring a detective. After that, we'll get out of your hair."

"Okay."

He'd given in amazingly easily, she thought, mildly piqued. Apparently during the night he had become eager to get rid of them.

"Do you have someone specific in mind to hire?"

"Not really. Believe it or not, I've never had an occasion to hire a private detective. But then, that's why Yellow Pages were invented."

"To look up detectives and sperm banks?"

She shot him a glare.

He chuckled. "Sorry. I couldn't resist. At any rate, when you get this detective, where are you going to tell him to start?"

"Start?"

"Yeah, he's got to have a trail to follow, and so far I don't think we even have the *beginning* of a trail."

She sighed. There he went again. *We.* This time she didn't even try to correct him. She was fast learning that as well as being compelling and fascinating, Ben was also like a train, hard to stop once he got going.

Except when he was kissing her. *Then* he could stop.

Suddenly she groaned. "Oh, Lord, I just thought of something. My *car.* The police will find my car with its window smashed and send out a missing person's alert for me."

"They won't find your car, Daisy."

"Why not?"

"If those men are the pros I think they are, they hot-wired your car and drove it off somewhere."

A chill settled over her. "Pros? Would pros smash my car window? I mean, wouldn't they do something with more finesse?"

"They got into your car the fastest way there is. And count on it, Daisy, they don't want the police looking for you. *They* want to be the ones who find you."

"How very sinister sounding," she said faintly.

"I'm afraid it could be exactly that." He sipped his coffee. "Tell me something, do you have a normal routine?"

"Of course. Well, normal to me." The baby had finished his bottle, and she shifted him up onto her shoulder and began rubbing his back. She'd seen it done somewhere, maybe on television. At any rate, he seemed to like it.

"I mean, is there somewhere you're definitely supposed to be in the next few days? In other words, how long do we have before someone notices that you're not where you're supposed to be and gets worried?"

"It will probably be three or four days." The thought sobered her. Normally she and Caleb talked several times a day, but since he'd been on his honeymoon they had spoken only sporadically. And everyone was so used to her coming and going as she wished, it would indeed be a while before anyone missed her. She frowned. "And would you please stop saying *we* and *us*?"

"I like the way it sounds." The glint in his eye belied the mild tone of his words.

The baby gave an enormous burp and then began cooing enthusiastically. She turned her head to look at him, curious about what he could be saying, but his was a language only he understood.

"There are three things you need to find out, Daisy." Ben stood and began restlessly pacing. Surprised, she watched him. Restlessness was a radical departure for him. Since she'd known him, he had been so centered and calm. And sexy, definitely sexy—but then, that was another problem altogether.

"You need to find out who the baby belongs to, why he was abandoned, and who those two men were last night who were looking for him, and you need to do all of that as cautiously as possible. If you ask the wrong person the right question, you could be in a lot of trouble."

She tried to swallow, but found that the muscles of her throat had tightened. "I don't know who you are, Ben McGuire, but you certainly know how to sum up a situation and make me feel in over my head all at the same time."

"You *are* in over your head, sweetheart. You just won't admit it."

Sweetheart. The word had come so casually from him that she couldn't believe he had meant it as an endearment. More than likely he had called many other women by the same endearment. It didn't mean that he saw her as his sweetheart, and to protest the familiarity would be coy, a pretension she disliked immensely.

She had slept in his shirt, in a bed he was paying for, with him only a few feet away in another room. By accepting his help she had thrown herself into a highly intimate situation that had the potential to become even more intimate. Which was why she intended to take the baby and go her own way. Except . . . Ben kept throwing obstacles in her path.

Like common sense, which was hard to fight. And Ben himself, who was nearly impossible to fight.

The baby's head bobbed as he tried to twist around and see what was going on. She turned him and sat him on her lap with his back resting against her stomach. He stuck his fist in his mouth. She replaced his fist with his new pacifier, which he immediately took to.

"I'll admit I don't have a clue as to what has happened or what I should do about it, but given time, I can figure it out."

"And you don't want my help?"

"It's not that I don't want it—"

"What then? Is my company so objectionable?"

"Of course not." How could she explain to him that every minute she spent in his company felt as if she were being drawn deeper and deeper into a bottomless pit filled with pure fascination, a substance that to her mind was trickier and more dangerous than quicksand. "You know what I've noticed, Ben? I've admitted that this sort of thing is outside my sphere of experience, but it doesn't seem to be outside yours. So far you've known exactly what to do. I'm sorry, but I find that a little unnerving."

"Not comforting?"

Yes, she thought, it *was* comforting. And unnerving. "I'd like you to tell me once and for all what it is exactly that you do for a living."

"I see." His hard expression turned even harder. "You think a label is going to make you feel better."

"When you have very little to go on, a label can help. Why won't you tell me?"

"Maybe because I think a person is more than a label. And maybe because I've had a lot of labels put on me over the years and none of them really fits."

"What *would* fit?"

"I tell you what, *you* pick a label for me, whatever you like, whatever makes you feel better."

"You're not being fair."

"Funny, I would never have thought you were the type of person who would need someone labeled."

He was making her feel as if she had failed some sort of test, and she resented it. "Normally I'm not, but then, this isn't exactly a normal, everyday type of situation, at least not for me."

Almost absently he ran his fingers through his hair. Something was definitely bothering him, she reflected, and wondered what it could be.

"Look, why don't you get dressed—the baby should be fine if you put him on the bed. I have something I need to do."

"You're leaving?" The tinge of panic in her voice shocked her. After all, this was what she wanted, to handle the situation by herself.

"I won't be gone long, and then we'll have breakfast and go shopping. We're going to need clothes for you, plus a car seat for the baby and more clothes, formula, and diapers, that sort of thing."

She felt better knowing that he didn't intend to be gone long. And she also felt incredibly foolish for feeling that way. She still had a lot of unanswered questions about him, and it was a state of affairs she couldn't allow to continue much longer. One way or another, she vowed, she would have the answers soon.

After he left she returned to the bedroom with the baby and settled him on the bed, making sure the pillows created a secure space for him. He had turned over in the night, but it had seemed more by accident than design, and he hadn't gone far.

On impulse she picked up the phone and dialed Celeste's home number.

"I don't talk to anyone this early," came the muffled, cranky voice on the other end of the line, "unless it's a matter of life and death. Like *mine*."

"Celeste, it's me, Daisy. I need to talk to you. Wake up."

"*Daisy*. What are you doing up this early? Oh, wait a minute . . ." There was a muffled sound, and Daisy could visualize her friend pushing herself up in bed.

"Now—Daisy, are you all right?"

"I'm fine. Listen, I need to know if anyone came into the club last night looking for me?"

"As a matter of fact, yes. Two guys, very well dressed, very creepy. They asked for you by name and then asked about a baby."

"And? What did you tell them?"

"Nothing, of course. And when they got insistent, I had Mike—you know, the new bouncer—escort them out. The thing is . . ."

"What?"

"After they left, I got worried about you and called your house."

"You didn't leave a message, did you?"

"Yeah, I did. Didn't you get it?"

She almost groaned. If they had somehow tapped into her phone, or even had gotten into her house, then they would have heard Celeste's message and realize that they were friends. Celeste could be in danger. . . .

She caught herself. She had spent only a few hours with Ben, but already she was beginning to think like him—paranoid. That way of thinking came so easily to Ben. "No, I never went home. Listen, don't worry about a thing. I'm fine and so is the baby. This is all going to be resolved very soon. Just don't tell anyone anything, and if those guys come around again and bother you, call the police. Only leave me out of it. Okay?"

There was a long stretch of silence on the other end of the phone. "Well, now I'm *really* worried about you."

"Don't be. Talk to you soon."

Daisy hung up, checked the baby again, then darted into the shower.

In the lobby of the hotel Ben inserted money into the pay phone and dialed the home number of an old friend. If he remembered the schedule correctly, his friend should be about ready to leave the house for work. The phone rang once, twice, three times. *Come on*, Ben thought. *Be home*.

The phone was picked up on the fourth ring. "Hello?"

"Marty, it's Ben."

"Hey, Ben, what's going on? Are you calling from Mexico? How's the fishing?"

"I haven't gotten started on it yet. Listen, I need to ask you a question. Was Debra Norton there when you went off duty last night? And what about the baby?"

Marty let out a long whistle. "How'd you find out about that?"

"Find out about what?"

"The missus took the baby and vamoosed. The man's got us all on full alert. I just came home to shower and change. I was halfway out the door when you called. So how'd you find out? Do you know anything?"

More than I should, Ben thought grimly. "Listen, Marty, I need to ask you a big-time favor. Don't tell the man I called."

"You *do* know something. Dammit, Ben, you've got to realize that it's only a matter of time before he has us check on you."

"Start in Mexico. And I owe you one."

Daisy emerged from the bathroom, wrapped in a towel, and saw that the baby had fallen asleep. As she gazed at him she chewed on her bottom lip. She'd never been in the position before where what she decided would impact so strongly on another human being, in this case a tiny, completely helpless human being. A wrong decision might affect the rest of his life adversely. But what would be the right decision?

She had honestly thought a detective might be the answer, but everything Ben said made so much sense. She would need to give a detective a place to start, and at the moment she didn't have one. Not a safe one anyway.

Ben. Where was Ben? Wasn't it time he came back?

She picked up her watch from the dresser and with a glance at the time fastened it on her wrist.

According to her watch, Ben had been gone only a short while. She could think of no reason for her to worry about him. There was also no reason for her to be as eager as she was for him to return.

"Daisy?"

At the sound of his voice she hurried into the next room in time to see him shutting the door to the suite behind him. His expression was grim.

"What? What's wrong?"

"Daisy—"

He looked over at her and his expression stole her breath away. It was of hunger and need, raw and unmasked. Instinctively her hand flew to the top of the towel around her to hold it in place. Electricity arced between them, creating an acute awareness of desire—in him, in her. Time slowed, almost stopping. A million thoughts flew through her head, and all of them centered on him. She wasn't sure what was about to happen or even what it was she wanted to happen. . . .

Slowly, like a man caught in a dream, he walked to her. Without a word he lifted his hand and skimmed his fingers across one still-damp shoulder. Her womb contracted with a flash of desire, her pulses raced out of control.

She could feel her throat closing. "Ben—"

"Get dressed," Ben said harshly, "and then we'll talk."

Daisy felt deflated and empty, like a balloon

pricked with a sharp pin. She escaped into the bedroom and quickly slipped into the panties she had washed out and hung to dry in the bathroom the night before, and then into the red dress. Still shaken by what had just happened, she regarded herself critically in the mirror. Her eyes looked unnaturally bright and her skin appeared flushed, as if every emotion she possessed had risen to the surface.

She smoothed the red dress down over her hips and ruefully gazed at herself. There was no way, she realized, that anyone would view the dress as a simple sundress suitable for day wear. It was too blatantly sexy. She'd always thought of it as a fun dress, but now she couldn't wait to pick out something plain and nondescript to wear.

Slowly she walked back into the living area and found Ben in the kitchen, pouring himself a cup of coffee. With their last encounter fresh in her mind, she eyed him warily. "Okay, I'm dressed, now what's wrong?"

He took a sip of the coffee as if to brace himself with the caffeine, then set the cup down. "We need to pack up and leave here."

"Leave here? Why?"

"I had a hunch and I played it. I'm almost certain I know who the baby is."

She didn't really want to know the answer, she realized. She might be inept where taking care of the baby was concerned, but she loved having someone to care for. Because of the baby, her life had gained a badly needed purpose. But now she was about to learn the baby's identity and who he really belonged to. She didn't want to know, but she had no choice. "Who is he?"

"Do you know who Peter Norton, Jr., is?"

She blinked in surprise. "Of course." Peter Norton was a high-profile Texas billionaire who had been in the news lately, talking about his political aspirations.

"I think the baby in there"—he nodded toward the bedroom—"is Peter Norton the Third."

She felt the color drain from her face. "That's impossible. No one would leave Norton's child in my car, either accidentally or on purpose. His child would be one of the most well guarded in the country."

"Except from his mother. The baby wouldn't be guarded from his mother."

"What are you saying? That the mother kidnapped the baby? A mother can't kidnap her own baby."

"That's exactly what she'd have to do to get Peter Norton's son away from him. And I know for a fact that sometime yesterday the mother took Norton's baby and ran from his estate."

"No," she said, shaking her head. "The Nortons have a picture-perfect marriage, everyone knows that. And besides, if what you're saying even has a grain of truth, the entire state of Texas would be on alert and the news would be plastered all over the paper."

His mouth tightened into a grim line. "That would depend on *why* the mother took the baby."

"I don't understand."

"I know you don't, but all you need to know for now is that at least *part* of the state of Texas is on alert, the part that works for Norton, and no doubt looking for you because they know by now that you have the baby. And soon, probably within the next few hours, they'll start looking for me too. As for the newspaper—Norton would want to keep this as quiet as possible."

She shook her head again, unable to accept what he was saying. "Ben—"

"Daisy"—he took hold of her bare arms—"I promise that I'll answer all your questions once we're resettled. But for now, it's time for you to make another decision, maybe the most important decision you've made up until this point."

"What?" she asked, bewildered.

"You have to decide whether or not you trust me."

"Trust you?"

"That's it. Do you or don't you?"

"I—"

"No, don't think about it, don't analyze it. Just give me your gut reaction. *Do you trust me?*"

"Yes." She said the word before her mind had time to form it consciously. And because she did, she realized that it was the truth. Instinctively she did trust him.

His stance relaxed and his expression turned to one of satisfaction. "Then gather the baby's things together. We need to get out of here."

FIVE

Daisy had always longed for what she viewed as a normal life. She remembered one time asking Caleb if he ever wished the two of them could live like everyone else, fall in love, have kids, lots of them, so that their two families could have huge get-togethers. She'd pictured kids and dogs playing on the lawn, with her taking home movies and Caleb barbecuing something wonderful for them to eat.

He'd said that one day it would happen for her, but that he would probably come alone to her barbecue. His prediction hadn't come true. He had found someone and though whether he and Joy would ever live what most people viewed as a traditional type of life remained to be seen, they would be happy. Of that Daisy was certain.

As for her, deep down she wasn't sure a normal life would ever be possible, but that didn't stop her from longing for it. And the day that followed gave her a taste of what it might be like.

To anyone watching her and Ben, she reflected, it must appear as if they were husband and wife, a father and a mother taking care of their baby. They did ordinary things. Only the *reason* they did them was extraordinary.

She knew it was all only make-believe, but for minutes at a time she forgot. And for the rest of the time she studiously ignored it.

She was aware the situation wasn't good for her and that she had to be careful not to get too caught up in the fantasy. But even so she enjoyed it, perhaps too much.

Since she didn't have anything to pack, she took care of the baby while Ben gathered his things together and checked out of the hotel.

Their first stop was a discount store that had everything both she and the baby required for the time being, including a portable crib. For herself, Daisy settled on a couple of pairs of jeans, several T-shirts and changes of underwear, a sensible cotton sleep shirt, a pair of sandals, and a toothbrush, along with a few other incidentals.

In the end she also couldn't help choosing a few

items that weren't strictly necessary. There was a set of colorful plastic disks that struck her as just right for a baby's hand and a lovable, cuddly blue terry-cloth horse. And finally she picked an item that was more impractical than anything else—a small African violet with cheerful little purple flowers. She couldn't explain why she had to have it except that she simply liked it.

As she chose each item she tried to be mindful of the cost, but she still gulped when she saw the total. Ben, however, didn't even blink an eye and paid cash for all of it.

At the car they settled the baby in his new car seat in the back.

"I think we bought too much," Daisy said, casting a last critical gaze over the baby to make sure he seemed comfortable.

"I'd rather have too much than not enough," Ben said from the driver's seat.

"I guess you're right, but it never occurred to me that one tiny baby would need so much."

"Now you'll know what to do when you have your own baby."

Her own baby. Maybe, if she were very lucky, she would one day have her own baby, but for better or worse, at least for the time being, she viewed this baby as her own. Trey. Ben had told her the Nortons had called him Trey.

He was watching her closely, alternately sucking

energetically on his pacifier and making sweet little baby sounds. Leaning close, she smiled at him. "What a good boy you are, Trey." Her voice was soft, meant only for him. In response he cooed, lost his pacifier, and began waving his arms excitedly in the air as he tried to grab her hair. Her smile broadened.

Still smiling, she glanced at Ben and was surprised at the strangely thoughtful expression on his face. It was the same expression he had worn the night she had brought the baby into the club and ultimately refused to contact the authorities. She hadn't known what he was thinking then, just as she didn't know now.

When he didn't say anything she forced her gaze away from him and returned her attention to the baby. She replaced his pacifier in his mouth and shut his door.

As she slid into the front seat beside Ben, his gray eyes flicked over her, causing heat to spread across her bare skin. She had no idea how he could make her feel as if he were touching her. Even more alarming, at times like this she wasn't sure it mattered that she didn't. The result was what seemed important. Along with her continued wariness.

"Why do you carry so much cash?"

He shrugged. "It's just habit."

"You have strange habits. Most people carry traveler's checks. They're safer."

"They're too much trouble. Besides, I've never had any problem with losing cash or having it stolen."

Unconsciously she squared her shoulders. "I want you to know that I plan to pay you back every cent."

Humorous glints joined the heat in the depths of his gray eyes. "If you like, but I enjoyed doing it. Besides, I would have thought you'd be used to men buying you things, though probably from Tiffany's instead of a discount store."

Her nerves tightened, and she clasped her hands together in her lap. Upset that he could get to her so easily, she said, "That's a huge leap of assumption, and absolutely wrong."

"Good. I'm glad to hear it." A smile touched his hard lips, softening them.

"Why?" Her gaze was drawn to his lips. *Desire*. She remembered all too well that when he had kissed her last night his lips had tasted like desire.

"Because I don't like the idea of another man buying you things."

Catching her off guard, he leaned toward her and pressed his mouth to hers. Given in broad daylight in the busy parking lot of a discount store, the kiss was startlingly intimate and strongly possessive. His tongue played with hers, lazily but surely, learning and experimenting with texture, with taste, with technique that made her bones heat clear through and go soft. His long fingers combed through her hair and tangled in the waves. His kiss brought heat and desire to her . . . and gave her a small sample of something she was beginning to want more and more.

She clenched her hands tighter together, fighting her feelings, but then found herself lifting her hand to his face and touching his smoothly shaven skin. She inhaled and smelled the soap-clean smell of his skin. She was drowning. . . .

But then he drew away and she had to stifle the urge to cry out.

"Thank you for trusting me," he said in a husky whisper. "You won't be sorry."

Whether she would be sorry or not was highly debatable, she reflected ruefully. Her trust was restricted to the situation involving the baby. Where she and her personal feelings were concerned she didn't trust him one bit because he could make her feel emotions and sensations she had never before felt, emotions and sensations that were at odds with her plan for her life, a plan that made sense to her. The feelings Ben engendered in her did not make sense. She couldn't contain or control them, and therefore she viewed both the feeling and Ben with suspicion.

As she was thinking that, he smoothed a thumb across her bottom lip, soaking up the moisture he himself had put there with his lips and tongue. Heat crawled across her skin, and she gave a silent curse because despite her suspicion she wanted him to kiss her again.

But he didn't. Without a word of explanation he straightened and started up the car, and Daisy was left to try to put herself back together again.

She propped her elbow on the window and put her hand over her mouth, willing her lips to stop tingling and her insides to cool.

And she wondered at his words. It was an odd thing for him to say, thanking her for her trust. If he had been any other man, she would have expected protestations of desire after such a kiss, but not once since she had known him had he conformed to what she had expected. And so he had spoken of trust instead of desire, and she was left aching.

As they drove, Trey made funny little gurgling sounds. Obviously he liked riding in a car, she thought, turning to check on him often. And proving his contentment, he eventually quieted and fell asleep.

Ben had brought the morning paper with him and had circled several ads for apartments to rent, explaining that an apartment would offer more anonymity than a hotel.

Daisy sat in the car with Trey while Ben went into three apartments, thoroughly checking each one out against some private list of his own. Finally, after a prolonged inspection of the fourth apartment and its complex, he came back to the car and with his hand resting along the top of the open door, he bent down so that his gaze was level with hers. "This is the one. It's large enough so that people move in and out of here all the time. We shouldn't cause too much undue interest. I've given the manager the first and last month's deposit for a unit on the back corner of the complex that will allow us to come and go as we like without being seen. I've also explained to the manager that I'm doing temporary business in the area and that at the last minute I decided I didn't want to be away from my wife and baby for even a month, so I brought you two along with me. He understood."

The idea of Ben being a devoted husband and father bothered her because she could see it so clearly. She already knew how good he could be with a baby. And he could be even better with a woman. His kisses had the capacity to make a woman cling to him with desire, and his strength and self-possession created confidence in a woman. He would be a wonderful husband . . . for someone.

She frowned. "What about furniture?"

"It's furnished—nothing fancy, just a collection of stuff tenants have left behind over the years, but it's clean and has the basics. We can buy whatever else we need."

Something very close to fear trickled down her

spine. She would never in a million years have thought that merely acting in a fashion she viewed as normal would scare her, but it did. Or was it Ben who frightened her? Ben, because he effortlessly drew her and kept her by his side.

"I don't think we'll need anything else. It's not as if we're setting up housekeeping."

"No," he said mildly, and reached out his hand to her to help her out of the car. "But I want it to appear that way to anyone who's watching us."

"You think we're being watched?"

"You can never tell who might be glancing out a window and get a glimpse of us, but I don't think it's anything we should worry about. The important thing is to look normal."

Normal. There was that word again. Something she'd always aspired to be. *Except under these circumstances.* With Ben she was simply pretending, and in this instance pretending didn't seem good enough.

Suddenly he chuckled. "I've got to tell you that the sight of you in that red dress is anything but ordinary."

"I'll change as soon as we get inside."

"Fine, but I have a feeling the sight of you wearing those jeans and T-shirts we just bought will be enough to stop most red-blooded men's hearts."

Another compliment. Another few moments before her heartbeat returned to normal.

❦ ——————— ❦

"Okay, Ben," Daisy said later that evening. "It's time you told me what's going on. I want some answers."

He gazed across the small dinette table at her, thinking that he'd been absolutely right. In jeans and a white T-shirt she looked every bit as fantastic as she had in that red dress. She brought elegance and sex to the off-the-rack clothes. And her skin, free of makeup, glowed with health and the texture of satin. He couldn't ever remember having a similar reaction to a woman, and he wasn't going to be able to keep his hands off her. He simply wasn't.

They had just finished dinner that he had made for them after a quick trip to the local supermarket, and Trey had been put down, hopefully for the night.

All afternoon she'd kept busy with Trey, caring for, bathing, and playing with him. At his insistence she had taken over the main bedroom for herself, and they had turned the second bedroom into Trey's room. They had set up the portable crib at the end of the bed, and Daisy had put the African violet in the window in a position where she thought Trey would be able to see it.

She'd seemed content, knowing that they were safe, but the occasional frown he'd seen on her face had given him the distinct impression that she was trying to work something out. He'd known the questions would come. He just wished he could wait a little longer to give her the answers. . . .

"Ben?"

He exhaled a long breath. "Answers. Right. I've got a lot of answers, Daisy. The question is, do you really want to hear them."

"Of course."

"Really? Are you sure?"

"Why wouldn't I be?"

"Because, sweetheart, you're going to hate the answers."

"Yeah," she said softly. "I know." She'd been happy today, living in a self-created world where the only other two inhabitants were Ben and Trey, but she knew she couldn't continue to keep the real world at bay, no matter how much she might like to.

"Where do you want me to start?"

"That's easy. Since I understand why Norton's men would be looking for me—at least I do if those were Norton's men who broke into my car last night—"

"I can almost guarantee you they were."

"Okay, then why would they be looking for you? What would connect the two of us together?"

"Nothing. They're going to come after me

because they can't afford to leave any stone unturned and I'm a loose thread."

"Why? Why you?"

"Because I briefly did some freelance contract work for Norton, and when we parted company a couple of days ago it wasn't exactly amicable. Right now they don't have any real cause to think I'm involved, but sooner or later Norton will realize that his wife might have tried to come to me for help and that he'd better find me."

She sat back, colder than she had been a moment before. "And did she try to come to you for help?"

"Yes," he said, his eyes narrowing as he watched her closely. "She called me and asked me to meet her at the club last night, probably because Deep Ellum is one of the last places Norton would think to look for her. She's very much the Junior League type. Unfortunately it appears as if his men followed her."

Daisy felt the blood slowly drain from her face. "If you were at the club to meet Debra Norton, then you *knew* who the baby was. When I brought the baby into the club after I had found him, you lied to me and said you didn't know who the baby belonged to."

Quickly, before she could recoil away, he leaned forward and grasped her hand. "No, Daisy, I didn't lie to you. I honestly didn't know. I had never laid eyes on Peter Norton's son; not many people have. All I knew at that point was that the wife of a former employer had called and asked me to meet her there without telling me why." He paused and the expression in his eyes softened. "But then, while I was waiting, I met this dazzling redhead with the most outrageous line I'd ever heard and suddenly she—*you*—took precedence over everything. At that point Debra Norton hadn't showed and all it took was one look at you and I didn't particularly care that she hadn't."

"But I said good-bye and left and—"

"I had already decided I was going to find out who you were and where you lived. With my connections it would have been a piece of cake."

"Connections? Ben, I feel as if you're leading me into a maze made up of more questions. *What* connections?"

"I know a lot of people here in Dallas. I was raised here. I also know how to ask questions and manipulate computer systems so that I can find out practically anything. Please get that stricken look off your face. What I'm saying is not that menacing."

"No?"

"Listen to me. It's not that big a deal. I slipped out after you the first time you left the club and copied down your license number. I definitely planned to see you again. But then, when you came back into the club with the baby, it was obvious that you needed help and I—"

She tried to draw her hand away, but he held it fast. "Don't pull away from me, Daisy. I'm telling you the truth. I wanted to help you, but I also had no intention of letting you get away from me."

She stared at him, realizing that in some remote level of her consciousness she had known he had an agenda that had nothing to do with the baby, and that agenda was her. And she wasn't blameless. She'd agreed to let him help her because she'd determined that doing so would be in Trey's best interest. But she'd also agreed to let him help her because she had been and continued to be in some very elemental way attracted to him. "I see," she said faintly.

"Do you?" His expression was doubtful. "Do you know, do you *understand* that you are in no danger from me?"

"I would guess," she said slowly, "that would depend on my definition of danger, wouldn't it?" *He* was danger.

His eyes narrowed to slits. "If your definition is me, then change it, because I'm not dangerous to you."

"Don't underestimate yourself. You're able to slip out of clubs, copy down my license number, *and* read my mind. You're a very accomplished man." Looking away from him, she rolled her shoulders, trying to ease the tightness from her muscles. "Never mind. It isn't important. You said you are a former employee of Norton's?"

"It *is* important, but we'll drop it for now if you want." At her emphatic nod, he continued. "Okay, that's right. I worked very briefly for Norton as a security consultant."

"Security? But you said you were a jack-of-all-trades."

"I prefer to say that when I meet someone casually. Saying security work demands a lengthy explanation, and it's easier to simply use the term 'jack-of-all-trades' than wasting time explaining when I know I'll probably never see the person again."

"You didn't think you'd see me again?"

"With you I *knew* I would, or die trying." A blush edged upward from her throat into her cheeks. For a moment he was caught up in watching her skin change color, but then he went on. "It's just that at that point I was very concerned with not scaring you off."

"And you're not anymore?"

"Should I be?"

He didn't frighten her in the way he meant, she thought. But there were other ways. . . . "So you worked *briefly* for Norton?"

"I didn't like the way Norton did things, and we came to a quick, very loud parting of the ways."

"So why would Debra Norton contact you? Was there something between you two?"

"There was nothing between us. Less than nothing. I might have said good morning to her once, but I don't remember."

"Then why?"

"She was there when her husband and I had our final blowout. It's just a guess, but I may be the only man she's ever seen stand up to her husband and walk away whole. If that's the case, and *if* she did in fact mean to leave the man, she would feel she needed someone to help her."

"And that would be you. My, my, you should really get a card printed up that says Damsels in Distress R Us." She pushed away from the table and rose in one continuous graceful movement, then walked quickly down the short hall to the room where Trey slept and came to a halt at the doorway. Trey was what was important, she reminded herself. He needed her and she needed him and nothing or no one else mattered. She could still take him and get away. . . .

Ben came up behind her, but took care not to touch her. "What are you doing?"

Trying to take a breath that doesn't have your scent in it. "Making sure he's breathing."

"He's fine."

She gave a soft laugh that broke apart in the middle. "You know, Ben, you seem to know so much about children, and you never did answer my question about how. Now, what do you suppose I should think about that?"

"Nothing, except that at that point I found you a more interesting topic of conversation than me." He wrapped his fingers around her upper arm and turned her to face him. "I still do, Daisy."

The small hallway was shadowed, and the only sound she could hear was that of her own heartbeat. It sounded loud, too loud, in her ears. "Are you married, Ben, or have you been? Do you have any children?"

He reached out a hand to her hair and lightly combed his fingers through a recalcitrant wave. "I have no wife, no ex-wife, and no children of any age. I don't even have a dog, because up to this point I've traveled too much."

He couldn't know how familiar that sounded to her. Or how sad. "Then how do you know so much?"

"Between them, my two older sisters have six kids and when I was younger and in school I used to baby-sit quite a bit. See? No mystery. Nothing ominous."

She threw a last glance over her shoulder at the peacefully sleeping baby, then returned to the small living room. "If you didn't know who Trey was last night—even though you were supposed to meet his mother—how did you find out?"

"I don't believe in coincidences, and my common sense told me I should eliminate the possibility. This morning I played a hunch and called someone I know on Norton's security staff."

"And he told you everything, just like that?"

"He's an old friend of mine."

Silently she absorbed the information. "So I ran off with the son of one of the most powerful men in Texas, not to mention the country." She shook her head. "Well, that's just great, just great. And you were absolutely right. I hate your answers. Every single one of them."

"Don't worry too much about it, Daisy. It will sort itself out one way or the other."

Her gaze flew to him. "You sound as if you think it's going to be easy."

"No, not really."

He walked around her toward the couch so that she had to turn to keep him in her line of sight.

"Norton's a bully, but if it's done in the right way he can be handled. What we have to do now is wait for Debra Norton to contact us." He took her hand and pulled her down to the couch with him.

And suddenly the length of her body was pressed against his from shoulder to knee. She edged away, putting a few inches of couch between them. "You think she's going to call us?"

The disturbing glint of humor in his eyes conveyed that he hadn't missed the fact that she had moved away from him. The heat in his eyes conveyed the uselessness of her actions. "Eventually she will. Remember, she's on the run just like we are."

"But *how*?"

"She has my business card with my cellular phone number on it."

"What cellular phone? I haven't seen any phone."

Without looking away from her, he motioned toward a nearby table and the briefcase he had brought in with him.

Her brows drew together. "Why didn't you use it this morning to call your friend?"

"The phone is turned off—on purpose. I'm supposed to be in Mexico. If I answered the phone, they'd know I was still in the area."

"Mexico?"

"Yeah, I've got a place down there where I like to go."

"Go to do what?"

"Fish. Relax."

Her head was spinning. She had the feeling she was being given very important information, but she couldn't decipher it. "Okay . . . so if the phone is turned off, how can Debra Norton get in touch with you?"

"Eventually I'll turn it back on. I'll have to. I've been giving her time to get settled somewhere, but if you want the real truth, I was mainly giving us time."

"*Us?*"

"Yeah, Daisy, us. You and me. You wouldn't be with me right now if it weren't for the fact that you're so concerned with keeping Trey safe. The fact that you are has given me a window of opportunity with you that I might not otherwise have had, and I decided to take advantage of it." His tone was almost dispassionate.

She stared at him. "Why are you telling me this?"

"Because you're already aware that it's true, and I don't see any point in pretending."

"Sometimes pretending is good," she said, and at that moment firmly believed it. Pretending helped keep reality too painful to deal with at bay.

"It's good only for people with no courage. That's not you, Daisy."

"So you not only read minds, you read character traits too?"

"Yes. Do you have any idea how hard it is not to touch you?"

Before she could take her next breath, he reached out and entwined his fingers in her hair, bringing her closer to him. His eyes were dark and hot. She tried to swallow, but found her throat had gone suddenly dry.

"I wanted you the minute I saw you," he said thickly. "It's a wonder I've lasted this long."

"Whatever happened to getting to know a person through dating?" Under the circumstances, it was a stupid, inane thing to say, and she knew it as soon as she heard the words come from her mouth. But she was finding it hard to think straight.

"When we met last night, you didn't strike me as someone who was interested in a conventional date. In fact, you were interested in only one thing from me." His grin was almost feral. "But when you found Trey, it gave me a great opportunity, and I grabbed it."

"An opportunity for what?"

"To convince you to want *me* instead of only a vial of my sperm."

She jerked away, drawing her head back, dislodging his fingers from her hair. "I told you, I've changed my mind. I'm no longer interested in having you be a donor for my baby."

"Good," he said, his voice a deep growl. "See? We're making progress. Right from the beginning I had something more personal in mind."

Heat congested in her chest, making it hard for her to breathe. "Let's talk about something else."

"Sure. What would you like to talk about?" He sifted her hair through his fingers as if it were lengths of silk.

"Debra Norton . . ." She stopped and cleared her throat. "She's got to be out of her mind about the baby." She couldn't say *her* baby, because she couldn't bring herself to assign ownership of the baby she had grown to love to Debra Norton, the woman she knew only through the occasional photograph that showed her wearing the latest fashion and smiling adoringly up at her husband.

"You mentioned that you had seen those two men chasing someone earlier last night. I'm sure they were after her. She must have gambled and put the baby in a strange car in case the worst happened and the men caught her. She didn't want them to get hold of Trey."

"Yeah, but that was a *huge* gamble." She was feeling on more solid ground now. "She had no idea whose car she was putting him in. If I had reacted like most people, Trey would now be with authorities, and she would have a terrible time getting him back."

"She definitely got lucky," he said, still playing with her hair, "but then, she deserves some luck."

"You sound as if you're defending her."

"I just happen to know that her life has been anything but a day at the beach since she married Norton."

"I thought you didn't know her."

"I don't, but I know the man."

"So she married the wrong man. She should file for a divorce like everyone else, not place her baby in danger by putting him in a strange car and abandoning him."

His hand stilled in her hair. "I'm positive she didn't abandon him and that she never would have parted from him unless she was desperate."

Frustrated by his attitude, she stared at him. "You know what I think? I think it's really wonderful how she has you on her side. In fact, I'm agog with admiration for you both."

"Agog, Daisy?"

She tried to get up, but he caught her arm and pulled her back down, this time closer to him.

"If she wants me on her side, she has me on her side. But you," he said, his voice dropping to a low mutter, "you've got me whether you want me or not."

"I don't," she said softly, too softly. "I don't want you." She was crazy to stay this close to him, she thought, feeling the heat coil through her. Up till then the kisses he had given her had been amazing, but she had been aware that they had also been kisses he had kept well under control. His control, though, didn't hide the intensity of his fire, and with that fire he had the capability to burn straight through her defenses. Like now . . .

He brought his mouth to her ear, his warm breath heating her inside and out. "Yes, you do.

You want me almost as much as I want you. All you've got to do is admit it."

She was shocked by her response to him, but she wasn't frightened. She should have been though, because she was fast losing the strength to deny him anything. And above all else, she did want him. Her thigh was pressed against his. His virile scent was surrounding her. His craggy face was close to hers. Her lower limbs were aching, her breasts felt full, her beaded nipples were unbearably sensitive. None of what she was feeling at the moment made sense, but she was new to passion of this magnitude.

He tugged at the waist of her T-shirt and spread his hand across the bare skin of her midriff. The contact was searing. If she didn't put a stop to it, they would be making love soon, she realized. It was her decision, and if she did nothing, it would still be a decision. What was she going to do?

In a sudden move he lifted her across his lap so that she faced and straddled him and his rigid length pressed against the inseam of her jeans which shielded the soft, hot core of her own sex. And she *was* hot. Lord, she was burning.

"This is our night, Daisy," he said roughly, his eyes flaring with hunger. "No one knows where we are. The baby is asleep and safe. Let's take care of us."

He gripped her hips and moved her over him, and she gasped as a thrill of pleasure shot through her. Needing balance, she grabbed for him and her fingers found the steely muscles of his shoulder. "You make it sound so easy."

"It will be if you let it. You have no idea how I've had to fight the need for you." He framed her face with his hands and brought her mouth to his for a greedy kiss. "No one is going to interrupt us tonight." He kissed her again, this time sending his tongue deep into her mouth.

She felt as if he were *already* making love to her. "Trey—"

"Will probably sleep through the night—he did last night—and if he doesn't, that's all right too. But for now he's asleep and we're awake and I want you so much my teeth ache."

She was throbbing from head to toe. Her body was demanding relief. "Debra Norton? . . . "

"At the moment she's not my problem." He clasped her bottom and squeezed the soft flesh through her jeans. "My phone is turned off and I'll leave it off until you say turn it on."

"Me?"

"You. I'm giving you the power. Isn't that what you want in a relationship? Power?"

He slid his hand beneath her T-shirt and closed it around one swollen breast. Lord help her, either she was going to have to stop this and get away from him, or give in to the madness and go with the flow of the passion and discover where it would take her. Her mind felt as if mist had replaced reason.

"You think I want power?"

"You want only a man's sperm. You don't want the man. But guess what? I'm a package deal. You have to take all of me."

His statement partially cleared her head. "No, Ben, I *don't* have to take all of you."

His hand continued to caress her breast, and at the moment she found it beyond her capabilities to wrest away. Because if she did, the wonderful feelings would stop and she didn't want them to. Not yet.

"Last night you wanted me to be the father of your baby."

"I told you, I've changed my mind."

"Why? Because you know me now? And knowing automatically brings complications?" He took her nipple between his thumb and forefinger and rolled it.

"That's right . . ." The words caught in her throat and she moaned aloud.

"Why are you afraid of complications?"

"Of *what*?" Her mind had again fogged with passion.

"Last night I asked you what you had against old-fashioned sex, and you said too many complications."

What was wrong with him? Why was he asking

so many questions? "Hurt. When things become too complicated, someone always gets hurt and usually it's the innocent."

"So someone hurt you?"

"Not for a long time."

"But you *are* afraid of being hurt."

She was hurting now, she thought. She rocked herself over him, trying to ease the pain, then grasped his shoulders as immense ripples of pleasure washed over her. Lord, she was making the aching worse, making the wanting worse. "But . . . We need to stop. I can't, I won't have a baby with you."

"Relax," he said, his voice a deep growl. "Haven't you heard this is the age of safe sex? It's something I definitely believe in."

She tried to focus on him, tried to catch her breath. "B-but you said I had to take all of you."

His lips quirked and she couldn't help but stare at them.

"I admit it's a blow to my ego that you don't want me to be the father of your baby, especially when I was just getting warmed up to the idea."

The humor in his voice was as unmistakable as the passion. Her defenses lowered even more. He lifted and turned her and eased her down onto her back. Pausing only to strip off his shirt, he braced himself over her and the usually cold steel of his eyes appeared molten with fire.

"Tonight is only a start for you and me, Daisy. We have plenty of time. I plan to make love to you more than once."

How had things gotten so confused? she wondered hazily. It hadn't been that long ago that having a baby was everything to her. Now all she could think of was the man leaning over her.

"For now we'll have protected sex, because it's the right thing to do for a lot of reasons, not the least of which is that everything should be right between a woman and a man when a baby is conceived."

The funny thing was, she agreed with him, but she had the odd feeling she was about to violate an idea or a principle that was important to her.

He eased the zipper of her jeans down, parted the material, then pressed his mouth against the silk of her panties. The heat of his breath fanned against her skin.

"I want these clothes off you." He matched his words to action and tugged at her jeans until he had them off. Then he replaced his mouth on her panties, only lower this time, and when he breathed, the heat went clear through her.

She twisted restlessly, seeking more sensation. She had made her decision.

"I knew you'd be like this," he muttered, his mouth pressed against her. "Hot and silky and responsive. I can't wait any longer. I'll be right back."

She cried out and grabbed for him. "*No.*"

He paused to look down at her. "God, but you're beautiful." Then he was gone. She supposed she should take this time to rethink her decision, but even as the thought crossed her mind, she lifted her hips and slipped off her panties, then raised her torso to pull her T-shirt over her head. Her bra followed the other garments to the floor. And then he was back, naked, muscled, virile. She held her arms out.

He lowered himself over her and entered her with a deep powerful thrust. No preliminaries. No soft words. Just raw need and urgent desire. As he felt her close around him he gave a groan of satisfaction. Never had any woman held him so tightly, nor made him want so desperately.

Her hands spread over his back and her fingertips made indentations into his skin. He began thrusting in and out of her, hard, powerful strokes that she met without hesitation. Sensations deluged him, ecstasy swamped him. He'd known it would be wonderful, but his fantasies hadn't been able to come close to the truth. The sweetness was unbearable. Now he knew the true meaning of hunger. Now he knew the true meaning of love.

SIX

Sometime near dawn, when the light was turning pearl gray, Daisy came slowly awake. Comfortable, warm, she stirred and found herself held by the weight of a masculine arm.

Ben.

She was lying on the couch, her body spooned against his, her back pressed against the hardness of his bare chest, abdomen, and thighs. Listening carefully, she heard the quiet, steady beat of his heart. She could even smell the musk permeating their skin, the scent of passion and intimacy they had created in the night.

That same passion and intimacy must also explain how the two of them had managed to sleep so soundly in the relatively narrow space of the couch. They had been exhausted and satiated.

Their lovemaking had been too good to be believed, she remembered, the kind of lovemaking almost too exquisite to be borne, the kind she had never before experienced. Several times in the night he had brought her to climax, and amazingly each time had been more intensely gratifying than the last. And each time he had made sure to use protection.

Now, as the darkness of the night was fading, she acknowledged to herself how grateful she was to him for being so conscientious, grateful because as important as she felt protection was, she had the uneasy feeling that she would have made love to him without it. He had taken her to dizzying heights of need and want time after time until she had been weeping for him to give her relief. And he had, forcefully, thoroughly.

Jack-of-all-trades, security expert, lover extra-ordinaire. The list of things she was learning about him was growing.

In fact, she wasn't sure it would be wise to learn any more.

Taking care not to wake him, she slowly slid from under his arm and off the couch. Cool air touched her skin. Pushing back her hair, she glanced around for something to cover herself with and saw Ben's shirt lying on the floor where he had tossed it hours before as he hastily undressed. The simple memory of that heated moment made her temperature rise. Flustered and bemused, she scooped up the shirt and slipped into it.

In the bedroom where the baby slept Daisy parted the curtains to allow a slice of the predawn light into the room, then sank into a chair near the crib.

Even asleep the little boy fascinated her and in this instance he also comforted her. He served as a reminder of the reason she had allied herself with Ben and he also served as a reminder of the plan she had devised for her life that had nothing to do with Ben, the plan that featured her being a single parent of a baby of her very own. For her own sanity she needed to remember that plan.

She had known Ben such an incredibly short time, but already it seemed he filled every corner of her life. His scent was on her skin, his taste in her throat, she even imagined she could still recall the feel of him on her tingling palms. She couldn't fault either of them for their lovemaking— quite simply their passion had been too great— and thankfully there would be no permanent consequences.

She almost smiled when she remembered her first impression of Ben.

Conservative.

There had been *nothing* conservative about his

lovemaking. He had set her on fire and taken her into an inferno of passion. The two of them had created a world where nothing mattered but the satisfaction of their desire.

And she could understand why their passions had blazed so hot. In order to protect a helpless child they had been living a life of enforced togetherness and as a result were in a situation where their senses were heightened.

Last evening had been nothing more than an idyll in a strange place in the middle of a strange night where no one knew where they were.

But dawn was here now, and soon the reason for their being together would be over, maybe as early as today. And then they would go their separate ways.

She tried to recall if she had anything to do this day, but her mind was blank. On the other hand, Ben had his trip to Mexico. Did he have someone waiting for him there? Possibly. Probably. In reality he had a whole life she knew nothing about. The thought disturbed her.

Gnawing on her bottom lip, she deliberately turned her mind elsewhere. Trey. With emotion tugging at her heart, she tried to imagine a situation so severe his mother had felt she had to hide him in a stranger's car. Even after what Ben had told her about Debra Norton she was unable to conjure up such a situation.

Trey deserved better; *all* children did.

❖━━━━━━━❖

Ben found her in the smaller bedroom, lying across the end of the bed, laughing softly at Trey, who lay between her and the headboard, cooing and gurgling. He barely glanced at the baby; Daisy riveted his attention.

Wearing his shirt, she was all unending legs and long, sleep-tossed red curls. In the shimmering sunlight of morning she looked soft, womanly, infinitely desirable. *Damn*. He wanted her again. If it wasn't for the baby's presence . . .

He leaned against the doorjamb and crossed his arms over his bare chest. "Good morning." His voice came out a gruff rasp.

She looked at him, laughter from Trey's antics moments before still warm in her eyes. "Hi. Did we wake you?"

"No." He savored the emerald warmth for several moments, then glanced at the empty bottle of formula on the windowsill. "How long have you been up?"

"About an hour or so." She held out the set of clacking plastic disks to Trey that she had chosen for him yesterday and watched with delight as he grabbed them and began waving them around, his arms and legs working energetically. He was obviously pleased that he could make the disks clatter together so loudly. "There's some coffee on the stove."

"I know there is. I think it was the smell that woke me up." He paused. "Why didn't you?"

She sat up and ran her fingers through her hair, trying to comb order into what she knew was riotous disorder. "Why? There was no need to wake up before you were ready. We don't have a schedule to meet today."

He pulled away from the door and strolled into the room. With a shove he repositioned the chair so that it faced the bed and he dropped down into it. "But we do have certain things we have to do."

She eyed him warily. As soon as he had entered the room, a multilayered tension had slipped into her bloodstream. She had never known any man to look as sexy and virile as Ben did at that moment. His jaw was darkened by an overnight growth of beard, his chest and abdomen were bare and roped with muscles, his jeans were zipped but not buttoned. During the night she had become so familiar with his body that she didn't have to put forth any effort into imagining what his body looked like beneath the jeans. In fact, as she thought about it, her mouth began to water. "We're not on a schedule," she repeated, highly embarrassed by her response.

"Have you forgotten Debra Norton?"

She picked up the baby and brought him against

her. Holding the disks with one chubby fist, the baby reached for her hair with the other, babbling all the while. "You said I could make the decision about when to turn on the phone."

"That's right. I said it and I meant it, but when I said it, I assumed we'd turn it on soon."

Trey tugged on her hair, and she pressed a kiss to his head. "I just need a little more time."

His eyes narrowed on her. "Should I be getting concerned about you?"

She held the infant closer. Just holding him made her feel better. He was safe and she was going to see that he stayed that way. "I can't think of one reason why."

"Daisy, don't let yourself get too attached to him."

Her hand came up to cradle Trey's small head. He was making soft, cooing sounds as he twisted his little fingers in her hair, the disks momentarily forgotten. "I don't see how it's possible to stay unattached. Look at him, he's wonderful."

"I agree, but what you have to remember is that he has a mother and she thinks he's wonderful too. I don't want to see you hurt."

Unaccountably she felt as if he were attacking her. "Hurt?" She didn't understand what he was talking about, and his gray eyes were shuttered, making it impossible for her to know what he was really thinking. He could just as easily be making a reference to staying unattached to him as he was to the baby. And if he was, she wouldn't be surprised. After all, he'd said he wanted her; he hadn't said he loved her. "You don't have to worry."

"Daisy," he said, his voice softer now, "I can see what the baby has come to mean to you."

She gently untangled Trey's fingers from her hair, kissed his forehead, and lay him back down on the bed. "I'd have to be made of stone not to care for him, and I'm not."

"I can certainly attest to that," he murmured.

Sex. He was talking about sex, not love. She didn't regret what had happened between them; she couldn't. But she had to remember that soon this was all going to come to an end and they would go their separate ways.

He leaned forward, putting his elbows on his knees, bringing himself closer to her, scrutinizing her. "What's the matter, Daisy. What's bothering you this morning? Are you all right?"

"I'm fine."

"You're sure? I mean, last night . . ."

She looked at him, wondering if she had really heard uncertainty in his voice. "Last night? Last night is over and done with."

He stared at her for a moment, taking in the new lines of strain that had appeared in the last few minutes on her brow and the shadows that had grown in the depths of her eyes. "That's an out-and-out lie, Daisy. Why are you lying to me?"

"I'm not lying to you."

"Yes, yes, you are. We both remember vividly what happened between us last night, and we also both know that it's not over. I sure as hell still feel the same way, and I'm convinced you do too."

She shook her head, trying to shake off the effect of his words.

"If I reached out and touched you right now, I could make you moan with pleasure."

She shifted uncomfortably. "Bragging, Ben? Somehow I didn't think that was your style."

"It's not, but the truth is."

He moved, taking her by surprise, reaching out and slipping his hand between her and the baby and into the open neck of the shirt. He closed his fingers around her breast, then let his thumb and forefinger take possession of her nipple. Heat and desire slammed into her with a brutal force, and she had to bite her lip to keep from moaning aloud.

"See?" he said, his voice thick with his own desire. "God, Daisy, nothing is over. It's just starting."

She jerked away from him and shifted around until she was leaning against the headboard, well out of his reach, with the baby in her arms. And she was distressed to find herself shaking. "I'm not sure what you think you just proved."

She watched warily as he leaned back in the chair and crossed his legs, propping one ankle atop the other knee. The position put stress on the denim of his jeans, causing it to pull tight across his thighs, and she had to force her eyes away from the enticing masculine bulge near the inseam. During the night she had learned all too well the pleasure his virility could bring her. It was a night and a lesson she would never forget.

"Maybe I didn't prove anything. Maybe I just wanted to touch you so badly I couldn't help myself. Maybe I want to do much more to you and with you, and if it weren't for the baby, I would. And the truth is, Daisy, there's flat out *no* maybe about it."

She closed her eyes for a moment, trying to fight the heat that his words evoked. Where he was concerned she was hopeless, helpless. . . .

"What's the matter? Did complications raise their ugly head sometime between the time we met and now? What are they anyway, these complications you're so afraid of?"

"They're nothing. Absolutely nothing."

"You could have fooled me."

Only the clacking of the disks Trey was wildly swinging sounded in the charged silence. She gazed down at him because it was easier to look at him than it was to look at Ben. "Don't turn on your phone just yet."

"Give me a reason."

"Just don't." At her sharp tone Trey looked up at her. She patted his back reassuringly.

"You're putting off the inevitable."

"Only for a couple of hours more."

"But why?"

She was holding herself rigid, she realized, all her muscles tensed. She let out a long sigh in a conscious effort to try to relax. "I guess you're right. I have become attached to Trey. The thing is, he's so innocent and so helpless and his parents are going to try to carve him into two pieces for their own selfish reasons."

"Why would you say that?"

"It's obvious. The Nortons are headed for divorce and an inevitable custody battle. It'll probably get ugly, and Trey will be badly hurt."

"And you think you can keep him from being hurt?"

"I can certainly try."

"Daisy, the night you found Trey I listened as your friend Celeste told you that you weren't thinking straight, that you should contact the authorities. And I watched as you ignored her and dug in your heels about Trey. You were determined right from the beginning to protect him, even before you knew who he was. Where does that determination come from?"

"What possible difference does it make?" She laid Trey down, slid off the bed, and quickly arranged pillows around him. "I need a cup of coffee and a shower. Will you watch him?"

"Wait. Don't run out on this discussion just yet. It's important."

She swung around to him, her red hair flying. "Why? That's the part I don't get. Why do you even care what my reasons are? They're none of your concern. You've helped me and I'm grateful, but that doesn't give you any rights where I'm concerned."

He came up out of the chair and closed the distance between them. "What's the matter, Daisy? Am I treading on sensitive ground?"

"What you're doing, Ben, is being a damned *bore*."

He burst out laughing, a loud, uninhibited eruption of pure amusement that took her by surprise. Even the baby stilled for a moment at the sound.

"I don't think a woman has ever called me a bore before."

She believed it. "Then if you don't want to hear me do it again, drop the subject."

Quieter now, more thoughtful, he smoothed his forefinger down the side of her neck and back up it. "I don't care what you call me, Daisy, as long as you keep calling me something. I'm also not going to give up trying to figure you out." He moved closer to her. "And I sure as hell am not going to agree with you that last night is over."

She found herself staring at his throat in order to avoid his eyes, a compelling mixture of steel and fire. Behind her on the bed Trey resumed cooing and gurgling and energetically swinging his clacking disks, his plump little legs working hard. As she stood there, her mind discarded one thing after another that she could say to Ben. With him so close it was difficult to think rationally.

A knuckle beneath her chin raised her face so that she was forced to look at him. "Some people have a defense shield, Daisy. You have something equal to the Great Wall of China."

She'd never considered herself particularly defensive. In fact, the whole idea startled her. Pondering what he had said, she moved away from him and kept moving until she was at the bedroom door. "I'd appreciate it if you'd watch Trey for me while I take a bath." Without waiting for his answer, she headed for the other bedroom.

The heated water of the shower did little to assuage the surprising need that lingered in her body. Still, the time away from Ben did help clear her head. She deliberately slowed her pace and took her time, washing her hair and dressing slowly. Thirty minutes later, feeling refreshed, she walked into the kitchen area to find Ben cooking breakfast and Trey falling asleep in his infant seat.

"A nap? Already?"

"I think your play time with him tired him out, plus I gave him as much of the cereal as he would take. I was telling him about the great fishing in Mexico, when he just dozed off on me."

"I wouldn't take it personally. Give him a few years." She said it, then realized chances were excellent neither Ben nor she would know Trey in a few years. Saddened by the thought, she lifted the baby from his seat. "He'll probably rest better in his crib. I'll be right back."

Once again in the smaller bedroom, she gently and carefully laid Trey in the crib. Using rolled-up blankets, she propped him on his side, then nestled the little blue horse in his arms and drew a light-weight coverlet over him.

Lingering, she gazed down at him. Before he had come into her life, her contact with babies had been minimal, so of necessity her thoughts of having a baby had always been in the abstract. But there was nothing abstract about Trey. He was a living, breathing, fussing, smiling baby who was completely dependent on someone else to feed, change, and love him. . . . She never would have guessed exactly how much time a baby took. She never would have guessed how much a baby could take hold of your heart, *her* heart.

When she returned she gave the close confines of the kitchen a quick survey and decided against volunteering to help Ben. Instead, she grabbed herself a cup of coffee and retreated to the table.

Buttering a stack of toast, Ben kept his eye on Daisy. Her hair was damp and lay in dark red curls against the white of her T-shirt. Every once in a while she would move her head, causing her hair to slide across the T-shirt and leave moisture behind on the cotton material. In his mind he could see the skin beneath, the cream color, the flawless texture, the erotic fullness of her breasts. God, he wanted her again.

He dumped a skilletful of scrambled eggs onto a plate and set it in the center of the table. "I didn't know how you liked your eggs, so I took the easy way out."

"That's fine," she said without looking at him. "I don't eat that much in the morning anyway."

"This is liable to be a long day. You should eat." He made a couple of more trips to the kitchen to fetch bacon, toast, butter, jelly, plates, silverware, napkins, and finally orange juice.

Belatedly Daisy realized she was letting him wait on her. "I'll do the dishes when we're through."

He shrugged, then filled his plate. "If the baby's still asleep and doesn't need you."

"Even if he's awake, I want to."

His expression was thoughtful. "Have you given any more thought to turning on the phone?" The question was carefully asked.

She stared at a side plate of bacon, then reached for a strip and took a bite of it. "Yes."

"And?"

Her gaze strayed in the direction of the baby's room and the little boy who slept there. "We'll have to turn the phone on soon—I realize that—but I want to hear what the mother has to say for herself before I make any decision about Trey." He put down his fork and looked at her. "She put him in my car, Ben. She may have been hiding him, but she also may have been abandoning him. As I say, I'll make my decision after I hear what she says."

"And what about Norton?"

"If I have to fight him for Trey, I will. I'm not without my own resources."

"What does that mean? Money?"

"Money," she said succinctly, "and I won't hesitate to put it to use to protect Trey." More than a little curious about his reaction to her mention of her money, she waited. Ben was a strong, self-possessed man, and, she guessed, he wouldn't run screaming if a woman had more money than he. She wasn't disappointed.

"I don't care how much money you have, you wouldn't stand a chance against Norton. Not only does he have power and influence, he is the biological father."

"Biology doesn't make a father."

Fascinated and puzzled, Ben stared at her. Last

night she'd been a wanton in his arms, but when it came to Trey, she was completely serious and very determined.

"You know," he said, "you were complaining that you didn't know anything about me, but I could make the same complaint about you."

"I thought you didn't like labels."

"I don't, and I'm not talking about labels. I'm talking about the things that make you you. For instance, I know that you want a baby and that you are fiercely determined to protect Trey, no matter what. You say you have money. So, okay, fine, good for you. I assume you live here in Dallas. It doesn't seem as if you have a job. Men . . . what about men, Daisy? You obviously don't want one involved in the raising of your child, but last night you wanted me for something else."

The bottom of her coffee mug hit the table with a thud. "Be very careful, Ben."

He held up a hand. "You're right. I'm sorry. There's no way you were the only one involved last night. In fact, I was involved two hundred percent, a unique experience for me."

"Really?"

He smiled. "Yes, really. There's something between you and me, Daisy, and there's no use denying there is. Last night didn't get it out of my system, and I'm hoping like hell that it didn't get it out of yours."

Distractedly she ran her fingers through her still-damp hair, then blew out a long breath. "Okay, you're right and the truth is I'm having a hard time figuring out what's happening between you and me."

"I would say the answer is fairly simple, Daisy."

"Not to me. Maybe I could do a better job of figuring it out if I weren't so concerned about Trey and what to do about him, but until I know what's going to happen with him, I have to think of him first."

"I'm not asking you to neglect him."

"I know you're not. You've been wonderful with him, but what I'm saying is . . . I could handle what's going on with us a lot better if I didn't have to divide my attention."

"I just want to know what I'm up against, that's all."

"Nothing. Everything." She shook her head. "We're going too fast, Ben, *way* too fast."

"I don't think there's any other speed I can go with you, Daisy."

SEVEN

Daisy dried and put away the last breakfast dish. She had taken her time cleaning up. She was growing very fond of the little apartment. It was cozy and comfortable, and heaven help her, she liked the fact that the three of them were there alone and that no one knew where they were. No one had to tell her that she badly needed a reality check. She knew it all too well.

While she cleaned, Ben had showered, dressed, and gone out to get a morning paper. But now he was back and sitting at the table in the small dining area, reading the paper. Now and again, though, she could feel his gaze on her. He had retrieved his cellular phone from his briefcase and placed it in the center of the table. The question couldn't be more plain: *When?*

She supposed it was the reality check she needed, and certainly it was a question she couldn't ignore much longer.

After another few minutes he folded the newspaper and set it aside. "Why don't you take a break and have another cup of coffee?"

"Sounds good. I'm through anyway." She settled at the table across from him, her cup newly filled. "You have all the subtlety of a hammer," she said with a pointed glance at the phone.

A smile flirted at the edges of his mouth. "I didn't see any harm in getting it out."

"No, I suppose not." With a sigh she rubbed her eyes, trying to ease the vague ache behind them. As much as she wished it differently, she couldn't put off the inevitable any longer. It was time to stop living in the fantasy. It was time to let the real world back in. She dropped her hand from her eyes. "Okay. Turn it on."

"Are you sure?"

"I'm sure."

He flicked a switch on the phone, then leaned back in his chair.

She fiddled with her coffee cup, moving it an inch one way, then another, then returning it to its original position. "Do you think Norton has started to look for you yet?"

He shrugged. "Probably."

"You don't sound too worried."

"With the precautions we've taken, he'd have to get pretty damn lucky to find us this soon. I know we're all right. It's Debra Norton I'm uneasy about."

He was truly worried about Trey's mother, she realized. It had been a major concession on his part to hold off turning on the phone until she was ready. She wasn't sure why he had done it, but she was grateful. "Do you think Norton's men might have found her?"

"I don't know. I hope not." He held up a section of the paper and pointed to an article. "Did you see this? It's about Norton and his political aspirations."

She took the paper and scanned the article. "Wow, this is *not* complimentary." She checked the byline. "Matthew Stone . . . His name is vaguely familiar."

"You've probably read him. Stone has been covering Norton for quite some time. In fact, Stone is one of the reasons Norton called me in. The man's ultra paranoid, and he's convinced Stone is out to get him. One of the things he had me do was check every phone, fax, and modem line in his place for bugs. He also had me check all electrical outlets and appliances, plus the walls and ceilings of his house and the grounds."

"Did you find anything?"

"Just the bugs he has on his own people."

"His own people? You mean he tapes the conversations of his employees?"

"That's exactly what I mean."

"Good grief, what's he afraid of?"

"Of the public at large finding out what a brutal, ruthless man he is."

She stared at Ben. "Brutal and ruthless? Are you sure we're talking about the same person? Around Dallas Peter Norton has the reputation of being both a brilliant businessman and a civic-minded philanthropist."

"Which is how he wants to be known. He has the best public relations firm that money can buy behind him. Fortunately I think Matthew Stone may just have Norton's number. Judging by articles of his that I've read, Stone is an excellent reporter and one of the few people Norton hasn't been able to bribe or deceive. There's not a doubt in my mind that Stone is out for blood. Whether he'll be successful is another question."

"But Matthew Stone can't be the only reporter to see through Norton. If what you are saying is true, there must be others."

"I don't know, but Stone is the first reporter to openly question Norton's ethics, and I gather he's not getting too much help. Think about it, Daisy—it would be highly imprudent of the city of Dallas, not to mention out-and-out dumb, to take too kindly to a reporter who is metaphorically biting the hand that is feeding the city. Isn't the new arts center going to be named after Norton due to an enormous donation? Stone must be having a hell of a time getting anyone to cooperate."

Daisy nodded in absent agreement as she gazed at the photo of Peter Norton that ran with the article. It was the same formally posed picture that the paper usually ran. She'd never given it more than a cursory glance before, but now she studied it. The picture showed a handsome, successful man in his early forties. Nothing more. No horns, no evil leer, no sign of anything in his face to suggest undue cruelty or paranoia or anything else that might make a wife take their baby and flee.

A great many things had happened since that evening two nights before in X-S, and the list of what she didn't understand about those events was long. Sometimes she thought the answers didn't matter. After all, she had Trey. And Ben. Well, Ben was with her for now. . . . It wouldn't be so terrible if the phone didn't ring, she thought. She liked this little world they had created together, even if only the most fragile of materials had been used to construct it.

An hour later the phone rang.

Ben punched the on button and lifted the phone to his ear, but aware that it could be Norton or one of his men calling, he didn't say anything. It was always wise to let the other person reveal themselves first, and he would rather they think they had gotten a wrong number than hear his voice.

"Mr. McGuire, is that you? *Ben?* This is Debra Norton."

"Yes, Debra, this is Ben McGuire." He kept his eyes on Daisy. She was sitting cross-legged on a pallet on the floor with Trey, changing his diaper. And when the phone had rung she had visibly tensed.

"Do you have my baby?" Debra Norton asked anxiously. "Is he all right?"

"Yes, he's here and he's fine. We've been taking good care of him."

"Thank God." She drew a deep, shaky breath. "I've been so afraid. I can't begin to tell you how afraid. I was down at the other end of the block, hiding in an alley, when I heard what I thought was a car window breaking. I was hoping I was wrong, but at the same time I was scared to death it was the car I had put Trey in. I wasn't close enough to tell though. I was trying to get closer, when I saw you and a woman in a red dress drive away with him."

"The woman is named Daisy, and it was her car you put the baby in. You got extremely lucky when you chose her car."

She took another unsteady breath. "It was the only one that wasn't locked. I had no idea that Peter was having me followed. As soon as I got away from there, I started trying to call you and I continued practically around the clock. Thank God you turned on your phone."

"Having it off was a precaution, since I figured your husband would try to contact me. The longer he thinks I'm in Mexico, the better."

"You're probably right, but I've been out of my mind with worry. Mr. McGuire, will you help me?"

"If I can. Where are you?"

"At a motel north of Dallas. It was the most anonymous one I could find."

"Did you charge the room?"

"No. I've been saving money for months now. One of the few advantages of being married to Peter was that if you knew where to look, and I did, there was always cash lying around. I've got quite a bit saved, enough to get resettled somewhere and get a job."

"That's good. Don't charge anything. Do you know what your next step is going to be?"

She gave a small, sad laugh. "What I'd like to do is get Trey, put him in the car, and drive as far away from Texas as I can get. Maybe Canada."

"You might be safe there—for maybe a month. Then Norton would find you."

"I know." This time her laugh held even more sadness. "My husband's influence is far-reaching."

"Then if you know that, you must have a plan."

Daisy's beautiful lips were drawn into a firm straight line, he noted, and she was murmuring to Trey, soothing him, and at the same time, he guessed, soothing herself.

"I do have a plan. I'm going to blackmail my husband into giving me my freedom and letting me take Trey with me."

He let out a long whistle. "I hope you've got something good."

"I do," she said quietly. "I have something that would be very damaging to him if it were to get out."

"It damn well better be potentially cataclysmic, or it's not going to work." He looked over and met Daisy's eyes. Her expression was unguarded, showing vulnerability and hurt and exactly how hard this conversation with Trey's mother was on her, a woman in Daisy's mind guilty of reckless endangerment of the child she had grown to love in a very short time.

Trey was gripping Daisy's little finger in one tiny fist and was softly cooing. She had dressed him in a lightweight, one-piece, footed stretch outfit with snaps down its front. It was patterned with small pastel teddy bears, and he looked adorable. As he watched, she leaned down to whisper something to him. He grabbed at her hair with his free hand, but there was no doubt in Ben's mind that Trey was listening to her with rapt attention.

"Before you tell me what you've got, you need to talk to Daisy. If it weren't for her, Trey would have been placed with the authorities and you'd have to go through them to get him back. As it is, you'll have to go through her. Hold on." He extended the phone to her.

Daisy disentangled her hair from Trey's fist, slipped Trey's pacifier in his mouth, then rose and took the phone. "Hello?"

"Your name is Daisy?" Debra asked hesitantly.

"That's right."

"I can't tell you how grateful I am to you. I was so desperate, so frightened . . ." Her words trailed off as emotion choked her. "Trey is all I have. He's the world to me."

"Really? The world? And are you usually so careless with things that mean the world to you?" She couldn't keep the anger from her voice. She didn't know Debra Norton; but she adored Trey and things could have ended so differently for him if someone else had found him.

"I can imagine what you must think of me, but you've got to believe me when I say I never intended to leave him and I was never far away from him."

"Were you close enough to see me when I got into my car and found him?" Her tone was accusing.

"N-no, I wasn't."

"What would you have done if I'd just driven away? You didn't know whose car you put Trey in. I could have been a child molester for all you knew. You put your son at an awful risk, Mrs. Norton."

Silence stretched along the line. She noticed that Ben was looking at her with a worried expression, but she couldn't tell if the worry was for her or for Debra Norton. Only Trey seemed unaware of the tension as he lay on the floor, happily kicking and cooing.

"Everything you say is true, Daisy. Everything. I made a bad decision. In trying to save our lives I panicked and put Trey in danger, but I would never willingly jeopardize my son's well-being. And in this case the alternative—if it had been allowed to happen—would have been horrific. You'll never know how deeply grateful I am to you for spiriting Trey away from those men and taking care of him."

"What do you mean, you were trying to save your lives?"

Once again there was silence, but this time it didn't last as long. "I'm a battered woman, Daisy. My husband started beating me a year into our marriage. That was six years ago. He even beat me when I was pregnant. Oh, he wanted Trey, at least his ego did, but his rages would take over and—" Her voice broke. "And after Trey was born, I was in constant fear that he would turn his anger on the baby. He hated to hear him cry. I was afraid it was only a matter of time. I had to get us away. I had to. Don't you see? Can you understand what I'm saying?"

Fighting nausea, Daisy closed her eyes. She felt Ben take her hand and reassuringly squeeze. She opened her eyes and looked at him. He knew what Debra Norton had told her, she realized. Now she understood somewhat better why he had expressed sympathy for Debra right from the beginning. She gazed past him to Trey. Sweet, innocent Trey. She couldn't stand the thought of violence of any form being a part of his life.

"Mrs. Norton, I'm sorry for you and everything you've had to endure. I really am. But Trey is my main concern and has been ever since I found him in my car. You may be his mother, but there is nothing or no one who will make me give him back to you until I'm convinced he will be safe and happy."

"Making a life where he will be safe and happy is why I'm doing all this," Debra said, her voice breaking on a sob. "I can't stand to be away from him. I've been crazy with worry since I saw you drive away with him."

"I drove away with him because I didn't know who he was or whom he belonged to."

"I know. I know. But I want my baby back, I *need* him back."

"I'm not sure—"

"Listen, I have a plan that will make us both safe, one I need Mr. McGuire to help me with. And then Trey and I can start a new life."

Suddenly Daisy felt tired, and down on the pallet Trey had started softly fussing. "I'll put Ben back on the line and you can discuss the plan with him."

"No, wait!"

"What?"

"Tell Trey I love him. Please."

Without answering, Daisy handed the phone to Ben, then went back to Trey. Deliberately she closed her mind to the conversation Ben was having with Debra. She didn't want to think about Trey's mother and how much she missed her baby. She didn't want to think about the plans Ben and Debra were making so that Debra could be reunited with Trey. She didn't want to think about the time when she would no longer have Trey. And Ben would be gone from her life . . .

Her head began to ache with all the things she didn't want to think about.

She lifted a softly crying Trey against her and pressed a kiss to his soft cheek. "Poor little one," she whispered. "I don't blame you for being upset, having to be cooped up in this apartment. How about a change of scenery?"

Without bothering to check with Ben, who was

still talking earnestly on the phone, she took Trey outside to the small patio area, where one plastic-webbed lounge chair sat. She laid a blanket over the webbing, then eased herself and him down onto it with her legs stretched out in front of her.

Sunlight slanted through the branches of tall oak trees, warming them. Since the apartment was on the back side of the apartment complex, street noise was only a distant sound. Not too far away from the edge of the patio pink and red bougain-villaea blanketed a flower bed.

"See the pretty flowers, Trey?" She held him in the crook of her arm and pointed. Happy now, he gazed up at her and sweetly cooed. She gave him a swift but gentle hug. "How am I ever going to give you up? Will you please tell me that?" He reached up with a tiny hand and tried to grab her hair. She diverted his interest with the plastic disks, then watched him a few minutes as he alternate-ly chewed on them and waved them around. She mustered a smile for his antics, but sadness laced her words. "If things work out and your mother gets you back, you probably won't even remember me, will you?"

"Just because you return him to his mother doesn't mean you won't be able to see him from time to time."

Ben's voice brought her head around. He was leaning against the jamb of the open door, gazing down on her. "How long have you been standing there?"

"Long enough to decide that the sight of you with a baby in your arms is one of the most beautiful I've ever seen. Trey adores you."

"But he won't remember me."

"How do you know?"

"He's too young. But then, I'm not convinced yet that Trey *should* go back to his mother."

"I know you're not, but he should. All we have to do is fix it so that it will be safe for him to be returned to Debra."

"*We?* Really, Ben? *We?*" She readjusted Trey so that he was stretched out on the lounger on his back with her legs on either side of him, protecting him from a potential fall. She slipped the pacifier in his mouth and made sure he had a firm grip on his disks. He angled his head so that he could still see her, and smiled. The pacifier fell out of his mouth and she put it back in.

Ben pushed away from the door and walked to the foot of the lounger. "Bring him inside. We'll talk in there."

"I like it out here. The sun feels good. Trey likes it too." She'd never heard herself sound so cranky, she reflected morosely, but then, she'd never in her life felt as cranky as she did at that moment.

"Dammit, Daisy—" Abruptly he stopped and studied his surroundings. No one was around. Since it was the middle of the day, most people were at work or at school. "Okay, we'll do it your way." He vanished into the apartment and then reappeared with one of the dinette chairs. He planted it squarely beside her and sat down. "So, okay, Daisy, what's wrong?"

"What could be wrong?" Just then a gust of wind blew across the patio, sending her hair streaming over her face. She pulled the wayward red strands away and tucked them behind one ear. Sucking on his pacifier, Trey watched her.

"I'm sorry this is all so hard for you."

The sincerity in his voice made her look at him. Warmth and genuine concern shone from his eyes. Something in her heart stirred. "You think I should turn over Trey to her without even a question, don't you? You think by not doing so I'm playing God."

"I wasn't thinking that at all, Daisy."

"Then what?"

"I think you have your reasons."

With a sigh she looked down at Trey. The warm air was making him drowsy, and his eyes were growing heavy. She reached out and gently patted his tummy. "When I was four years old my mother and father separated. They violently hated each other, and it seemed to me that they hated me even more."

"Why would you think that?"

"Actually I should have left out the word *seemed*. It was really true. I figured out why when I got older. *I* was evidence that they had once been stupid enough to think that they loved each other, and when the dust settled, I ended up being nothing more than a trophy for them that each wanted to win only because they knew it would hurt the other. The court case dragged on for several years, with each year progressively worse. I had to take batteries of psychological tests, talk to case workers, and endure blatant bribes from both my parents. The court finally awarded me to my mother. I never saw my dad after that, and my mother fast lost interest in me. Thankfully the next time she married, she married into a family that provided me with a cousin. Caleb. We were both neglected children. Our friendship saved our sanity."

"I'm sorry."

She shrugged. "I have only the memories now, but they're strong enough to make me want to protect Trey from the same thing happening to him."

"His mother truly loves him. She's desperate to get him away from his father, and once she does she won't lose interest in Trey. He's the most important thing in her life."

Her instinct was to lash out with a sarcastic remark about the choices Debra Norton had made in her life, both with her husband and her son—after all, she had managed to lose her son. She drew in a deep calming breath and reminded herself that she had to at least try to be fair. "If what she told me was true, then I can understand why she'd want to get away from her husband."

"Oh, it's true all right. Remember when I told you that she was there when Norton and I had our final blowout? That blowout was about her. I was passing by his study one day last week when I heard her screaming. I rushed in and saw him striking her, and I stepped in and stopped it."

"And?"

"And it would be an understatement to say that he didn't take it too well. That's when we parted company. I told him I would not work for a man who used his wife as a punching bag, and I told his wife she should get the hell away from him immediately, and then I walked out."

"And?"

"Norton didn't say a word."

"How did she get your business card?"

"I slipped it to her. I was hoping she'd call for help."

"And she did."

He nodded. "Now that she's out of that house, we have to make sure she *stays* safe."

"Wasn't there anyone else around her willing to help her?"

"I'm not sure all his employees know, and I guess those who do like those big paychecks Norton signs for them too much to rock the boat. The worst of the lot is his political adviser. He's a real charmer. His advice to Debra has been limited to having her add an extra layer of makeup to her bruises to hide them for photographs and appearances."

A chill stole over Daisy. She couldn't even begin to imagine what Debra Norton's life had been like. "Okay, so she's away from him. What's going to happen now?"

"She's out of his clutches—*temporarily*. But I'll guarantee you that if he has his way, he'll get both her and Trey back."

"He won't get Trey back."

"That's what we're going to try and make sure of."

"No, Ben! I'm telling you! He's not going to get Trey!" Her outburst disturbed Trey's nap. Without opening his eyes, he screwed his face up as if he were about to cry. She reached out and patted him until he relaxed again.

Ben eyed her thoughtfully. Now he better understood why she had been so adamant about keeping Trey out of the legal system, but he had a feeling it might take a lifetime to truly understand her. But as it happened, he had a lifetime. "Okay, here's the deal. Debra has a videotape of Norton beating her, and she's—"

"Wait a second. How did she get a videotape of something like that?"

"She set it up."

It took a whole minute for the meaning of what he had said to sink in. "You mean? . . ." The idea was so horrific, she couldn't even say it.

"She set up a video camera in their bedroom at an angle so that it took in most of the room. She made sure it was hidden, then deliberately did something she knew would incite Norton to beat her. Daisy, she was that desperate."

She felt sick to her stomach. "The poor woman."

"It was the only way she knew to protect herself and her son. Because of who Norton is, it took a tremendous amount of courage to even *think* about leaving the man, and then to purposefully provoke him took even more. He could have killed her."

Bile rose in her throat, but she fought it down. She looked at Trey sleeping so peacefully in the afternoon sun, and for the first time she realized how much his mother must love him. She had grown to love him in the short time they had been together, but Debra had carried him in her body, given birth to him, loved and cared for him every moment of every day since he had been born, and had ultimately been willing to sacrifice herself for him. She could not, would not, judge Debra Norton anymore.

"Okay," she finally said, "so how is she going to use the videotape?"

"She's not. I am."

"Why you?"

"Because Peter Norton is a control freak who has completely ruled her life for the last six years, and he will move heaven and earth to try to change her mind and get her to come back to him. He's not going to believe that she'll use the tape, no matter how much she tries to convince him, and he's not really going to believe that she'll stay away from him. He'll throw everything he's got into changing her mind, and in the meantime he won't let up for a minute trying to get his son back. He's a master manipulator."

"So you're going to act as an intermediary?"

"That's right. In a little while I'll call Norton and set up a meeting."

"When?" Her gaze went to Trey. She was going to have to give him up soon, and her heart was already breaking at the thought.

"I talked Debra into waiting until tomorrow."

"Why?"

"I wanted Norton to have time to get nervous."

"Do you think an egomaniac like him will have enough sense to get nervous?"

"Not in the way most people would, but the longer things are out of his control, the more anxious and irritated he's going to become. Even if he's only a little bit off balance it will work in our favor." He paused. "I also wanted to give you more time with Trey."

"No matter how much or how little time I have with him, giving him up is going to be hard."

"I know and I sympathize. You had made up your mind that you wanted a baby and then you went out to your car and found one. It must have seemed like the ultimate wish fulfillment."

"Yeah," she said softly. "But even while I was falling head over heels in love with him, a part of me knew it was all too good to be trusted."

"All? Not *all*, Daisy. Only the part concerning Trey."

"What else is there?"

"You and me. There was one other reason I wanted to set the meeting with Norton for tomorrow. I wanted to give myself more time with you."

He couldn't get too much plainer than that. She stirred uncomfortably. "Look, just because last night we—"

"Made love," he supplied helpfully.

"Had sex. It doesn't mean that it's going to happen again."

"I realize that. And I don't believe I said anything about either making love or sex. I said I wanted to give myself more time with you, and that's exactly what I meant."

More time. One more night. One more night to be with Ben . . .

EIGHT

"I assure you, Norton," Ben said, speaking into the telephone later that day, "Debra will do whatever she has to do to get her and her baby away from you."

Listening to Ben's side of the conversation chilled Daisy to the bone as she sat in the living room. She'd never heard Ben's voice so cold or so hard. She'd never seen him so plainly and unmistakably in command, so unblinkingly formidable and merciless. She tried to imagine what it would be like if she were on the receiving end of that tone of voice and couldn't. With her he'd never even come close.

"And more than that," he said, continuing, "I'm committed to the same purpose. I guarantee you that the tape, if made public, will shoot your political aspirations down in big, bright flames. Now, you may not believe that Debra has the guts to make the tape public, but you had better believe that I do and that I will. I've already told you what I think of your abuse of your wife. It would make me extremely happy to tell the media."

Silence ensued as Ben listened. Daisy saw a muscle flex in his jaw. "You're not going to talk or buy your way out of this one, Norton. You're also not going to bully your way out. You've got to make a decision about how important your career and public image is to you. If it's as important as I think it is, then you had better do what I say."

Ben was quiet again as the other man talked. "Debra is safe and so is Trey, I told you that. Finding them isn't going to help you. I've got the tape and I've made sure that there's a copy of it in a third party's hands, a party who answers only to me and not to Debra. That third party also has explicit instructions as to what to do with that tape if either Debra or I are harmed in any way, so you had better hope that our guardian angels are working overtime." He paused, listening. "You can call me every name in the book, Norton, and it won't change a thing. And of course I realize you'll want to see the tape, but understand that it will be a *copy* of the tape. The original will stay safe. Tomorrow, Norton, at four o'clock in the afternoon. Meet us at the North Park Shopping Mall by the fountain at the indoor entrance to Neiman-Marcus."

His face split into a grin, and watching him, Daisy decided it was the same type of grin a predatory animal would have on its face right before it pounces on his prey.

"You know where that is, don't you, Norton? It's where a great many of your constituency shops."

Outside the small apartment, the afternoon shadows lengthened as evening crept closer. Inside, Daisy spent most of her time with Trey. She was getting used to taking care of him. Where he was concerned she was more sure of herself. She knew what to do when he fussed. She knew what to do to make him happy. She knew how much and what to feed him.

His mother knew too, of course. But could his mother keep him safe? The thought worried her. Debra deserved a new life with her son, but Trey also deserved a chance to grow up in a secure and protected environment. Would he get that chance with Debra? On the other hand, could she really in good conscience deprive Debra of her son?

And what about Ben? She wasn't at all comfortable with the emotions he aroused in her, emotions that could smash apart well-thought-out plans and destroy a person's peace of mind for an indefinite length of time. What was she going to do about him?

Ben puttered around the apartment and played with Trey when he could get him away from Daisy. He read, and to his satisfaction discovered another article in the paper by Matthew Stone on Peter Norton. Stone was getting close. He hoped the reporter would be able to tell the story he wanted to tell and come out unscathed, but unfortunately Ben knew Norton too well to believe that would happen. If he wasn't so busy trying to make sure Debra and Trey remained safe, he would give Stone a helping hand. But for now they came first. And Daisy came even before them.

He went out and bought food for their dinner. He watched Daisy. He had spent years living out of strange apartments, and here he was in yet another, but this time there was a difference. This time there was Daisy.

She had become all-consuming to him, all-important. He couldn't think of any other place he'd rather be than with her in this small apartment. Watching her doing even the most mundane things had almost become an obsession with him. He hated it when she moved out of his line of sight for even a minute. Her presence brought warmth to a room, life. Spending time with her soothed him. It also excited him. Quite simply, he loved her, and his mind was constantly filled with thoughts of how he could keep her by his side for the rest of his life.

Ben looked up from the book he was reading as Daisy strolled into the living room. "Trey asleep?"

She nodded. "With luck he'll sleep the night through."

"I'm sure he will. He did last night."

The idle comment made her remember. Last night they had made love. She combed her fingers through her hair, pulling it back from her face. "Poor little guy. He has no idea of all the turmoil that's going on around him."

"Which is how it should be."

She studied him for a moment. "You lied to Norton about having the tape, didn't you? And also about the third party."

His eyebrows shot up. "Does my lying to Norton bother you?"

"No. The man is pure scum. I guess I was just curious about the ease with which you handled him."

He shrugged. "I'll have the tape tomorrow, and shortly after that there will be a copy in a third person's hands, someone I know I can trust implicitly."

"Who would that be?"

"Actually I have several close friends who fall into that category, and fortunately I've taken precautions over the years to make sure no one could connect me to them."

"You mean you have friends no one knows about?"

"That's right."

"That's very weird, Ben."

His lips twitched. "Yeah, I know."

She folded one long leg beneath her and sank into a chair that was at a right angle to the couch where he was sitting. "But why would you do that?"

"Because of the work I used to do."

"Which was?"

"I used to work for the government." He held up the western he had been reading to show it to her. "Which is why I like reading westerns like this instead of political thrillers."

"Funny, I would have definitely figured you for a political thriller–type reader."

"Nope. They're simply not my idea of fun, and besides that, I've yet to read one that has all the details in it correct."

"How do you know that? Were you in some sort of espionage work?"

He grimaced as if he had just had a taste of something bad, and set the book aside. His movements were slow. It was obvious to Daisy that he was giving careful thought to how he would answer her.

"Perhaps a better explanation of what I used to do would be to say I did top-level national security work." When she started to ask another question, he hastened to add, "Let's just say that the job I do now as a security consultant was mastered during the years I was an employee of the government."

Yet one more thing she had learned about him. "You don't like to talk about it?"

"Not really."

"Why?"

"Because my former position with the government tends to make people think that it's easy to put labels on me, and the labels they choose are always wrong."

"Give me an example."

"Spy."

She blinked. "Well, now, there's certainly a label for you."

"Assassin."

She swallowed. "Another interesting label. *Riveting* even. But you say those labels are wrong?"

"That's what I said."

"I have to say I'm glad to hear it."

His voice gentled, but his tension remained. "It was important work and I was very good at it. I did it for a long time until I just didn't want to do it anymore. Someday I'll tell you all about it if you like, but until then I'd rather you get to know me as I am today."

Something about his tension made her want to comfort him. "Ben, I liked you from the first moment I saw you." He smiled a genuinely sweet and at the same time extremely sexy smile, and her heart grew warm. "It's true," she said softly.

"The liking was mutual, I assure you."

The liking was there and so was the passion, yet she felt an incredible panic. Why? Because she knew instinctively it wasn't safe to like him too much. "You know what?" Her tone was as casual as she could make it. "I think I'll sleep in Trey's room tonight."

Before her eyes his demeanor visibly cooled. "Fine. Wherever you'll be most comfortable."

"Please don't take it personally. It's just that I think I'll be happiest in the second bedroom with Trey. You can have the other bedroom." Uncomfortable with holding his steady gaze, she looked away.

"*Happiest*, Daisy? Are you saying you would be *unhappy* if you slept anywhere else?"

She studied her hands in her lap. "I'm not sure. It's just that I've discovered something about myself these last few days. I love to watch a baby sleep. Well, actually I love to watch *Trey* sleep. And if things go as you expect tomorrow, this is probably the last night I'll get to spend with him. I thought I'd make the most of it, that's all."

The silence that ensued was so loud it drew Daisy's gaze back to Ben. Dark lights flickered in the depths of his gray eyes, recalling to her mind the idea of danger.

"You and I could make a baby together," he said softly, "one every bit as sweet as Trey."

"No." She shook her head to add emphasis to her reply.

"Your answer's no because you care about me."

It was a statement, not a question, and it compelled her to defend herself. "I think it's perfectly natural for me to have come to think of you as my friend. I've already told you that I instantly liked you, and since that first night we've spent a lot of time together. You've been a great help—"

"There's more to it than just gratitude and friendship, Daisy. A *lot* more. You don't make love to man like you made love to me last night simply because you're grateful or because you've spent a few days with me and have come to think of me as a friend."

"How do you know that? You don't know me. Not really."

He smiled. "Okay, if it will make you feel any better, call it wishful thinking."

She eyed his smile with distrust. In many ways it was the same type of smile he had had when he had been talking to Peter Norton. *Predatory*. "Let's get back to Trey."

"Are you sure he's a safe enough subject for you?"

"Sarcasm doesn't become you, Ben."

"Are you positive?"

No, she wasn't. In fact, he looked maddeningly attractive, lounging back in the easy chair, completely self-assured, with one leg crossed over the opposite knee.

"Getting back to Trey," she said with determination. "If I return him to Debra, are you positive he'll be safe from his father?"

"Norton is possessed with the monster of ambition and power. He has a great deal and he wants a great deal more. Once he sees for himself what's on Debra's tape, he's going to realize that he can't possibly afford to let its contents get out."

"But how's he going to see it?"

"He's got a VCR/TV setup in that limo of his, which I'm sure he'll have parked right outside the entrance to the mall. And when he learns what's on the tape, I can guarantee you that he'll go into one hell of a black rage. It's not going to do him a bit of good though. His wife is going to win this one." He smiled, clearly relishing the idea.

"I hope you're right."

"I plan to do everything in my power to make sure that I am."

She believed him. She had found out for herself these past few days just how valuable an ally he could be when a person was caught in a dicey situation. And Debra Norton's situation was more than dicey, it was flat-out perilous.

A short time later she excused herself and went to the bedroom that had been designated Trey's. Troubled, edgy, she changed into the oversize sleep T-shirt and settled down near the foot of the bed so that she could be as close to him as possible. By the light of a small bedside lamp she watched him. The blue horse lay next to him, and he breathed softly and easily. The sight of him sleeping so peacefully soothed her ragged nerves. She wasn't sure she could ever rationally or logically explain the connection she felt to Trey, but he had become very important to her in an incredibly short time. Just as Ben had.

She thought of Caleb, somewhere in Europe on his honeymoon. From a very early age he had been a stabilizing force in her life, making her world right when adults threatened to send it spinning off its axis. And now she was the adult, trying her best to keep Trey's world stable for him, not to mention her own. She went back over the decisions she had made in the past few days, and amazingly she realized that she didn't regret a one.

She had no idea how she would go about explaining Ben to Caleb. What would she say? That she had tried to obtain a vial of sperm from a strange man she had seen in a Deep Ellum club and then proceeded to accept his help when she took the baby of one of the most powerful men in America and ran?

Come to think of it, if anyone would understand, it would be Caleb. He was a free thinker who had never let convention fence him in. The problem was, she wasn't sure *she* understood.

Sometime later she heard Ben walk down the hall to the other bedroom. She listened as he moved around, preparing for bed, and then the apartment fell quiet.

She rolled over on her back and covered her eyes with her forearms. She was doing the right thing by sleeping separately from him tonight, she assured herself. She was. So why, then, did she ache in every part of her body for him? And why did she long to feel his strong arms around her once more?

She stifled a groan of frustration. If it was true that this would be her last night with Trey, it was also equally true that this would be her last night with Ben. And Lord, but this last day had gone fast. Too fast.

Time was flowing through her hands like water. She couldn't stop it or contain it. There was a desperation in her, a feeling that there were still things she needed to do, to say, to feel, to share. . . .

With Ben.

She slipped from the bed and walked barefoot into the bedroom he was using. He was propped up in bed, reading, his long legs sprawled out in front of him. He was wearing only a pair of navy print boxer shorts. Her heart slammed against her rib cage and her knees weakened. He looked virile, masculine, and incredibly desirable.

He turned his head and saw her. *"Thank God,"* he said.

And then, as if he had been waiting for her, he tossed the book aside, reached out for her, and brought her down to him.

And they merged together. Quickly. Easily. As if all along it had been meant to be.

He was everything she wanted at that moment: gentle and intense, passionate and compassionate, understanding and demanding. She explored his hard body, touching, tasting, and most of all, wanting.

He took, she gave. He took more and she gave more.

But not everything. She couldn't give him everything.

And he knew it. He knew it and he didn't like it. Not at all. Because at that moment, as he held her close, devouring her with his mouth, worshipping her with his body, he realized the full power and extent of his love for her.

Early on he had acknowledged to himself that

he loved her, but at that point the emotion had been too new for him to understand everything about it. He had felt only the possessiveness of the emotion, the incredible need to have her and to keep her by his side. Now he understood more. Now he understood the caring.

The knowledge came to him like a thunderbolt, and with that knowledge came the realization that he couldn't force or coerce her into giving more than she was ready.

So he accepted what she *could* give, which was a great deal. Silk and fire, softness and desire. Within boundaries she was free with him. And so he took, savoring her tightness, her heat, and anticipated the time when she would give him everything.

The next afternoon Daisy sat at the dinette table, holding Trey close to her as he took his lunch bottle with a single-mindedness that would have delighted her on any other occasion. But she had spent the past fifteen minutes listening to Ben talk with Debra Norton. Tension and anxiety gripped her; sadness overwhelmed her. She had no idea how she was going to get through the day.

At last he hung up the phone. He had been standing in the living room, gazing out the window, but now he came to her and sat down across from her. "I think we're all set."

"Debra is insisting on being at the meeting?"

He nodded, his expression thoughtful. "I would have been glad to spare her that if she'd wanted, but I honestly think it will be better for all concerned that she show up. Norton needs to see her strong. He needs to understand that she won't be coming back. And I think she needs to confront him one final time in an environment she *knows* will be safe. It will do her a world of good to see that she can come out on top of this and walk away."

"I suppose so. And she's going to bring a copy of the tape?"

"I'm going to pick her up at her motel, and she'll have the original with her. We'll make copies on our way over to the shopping center and I'll mail the original to myself at a post office box I have. It's located in Oregon and is untraceable. The tape will be absolutely safe. We'll also send out a couple of more copies. Additional insurance is a wonderful thing in a situation like this."

She eyed him curiously. "Even though you're retired from the government, you have retained a lot of that life-style."

"Some habits never leave you, especially when they're habits that in the past have kept you alive."

"But you *are* out of government work completely?"

"Completely."

Trey drained the last of his bottle. She lifted

him on her shoulder and began rubbing his back. "I wouldn't imagine the kind of life-style you've led—or even the kind you're leading now—would be conducive to having a good relationship with a woman."

His gaze was steady as he watched her. "You imagine right about my past. My present life-style is a very different matter though."

"But you said you travel a great deal."

"I do, but I'm willing to change that and stay in one place. In fact, I'd welcome it."

"You mean if you found the right woman."

He nodded, careful to give away nothing that might spook her. First he would see Trey safely back with his mother, and then he could concentrate on winning Daisy's love. "Yes."

"That's what I thought you meant." Trey gave a satisfying burp, then promptly reached out for a handful of Daisy's hair.

With a grin he held out his arms for Trey. "Here, let me take him for a while and give your hair a rest." He untangled Trey's small fist from her hair and bundled him against him.

She smiled at the little boy. "He doesn't hurt me—I have too much hair."

"I can understand his fascination with it. The color must attract him as much as the texture."

"More than likely it's simply because it's always within reach."

"Nope. He knows gorgeous hair when he sees it, I can tell."

"You can, huh?" she asked, secretly amused and flattered.

"Yep." He looked down at Trey, who returned his gaze. "I'm going to miss this little guy."

"You are?"

"Sure. You're not the only one he's managed to win over."

She studied the picture the two of them made, Trey, a tiny boy, held securely in Ben's strong arms. It was a nice picture. "Have you ever thought about having children?"

His smile broadened and a twinkle appeared in his eyes. "You mean children whom I'll have an active part in conceiving and raising as opposed to just a perfunctory part in the conception?"

"That's what I mean." The words came out sharper than she had intended.

Trey was gurgling and kicking his feet. Ben held his plastic disks in front of him and waited patiently. Trey swiped at the dangling disks several times before he managed to grasp one, which he then promptly brought to his mouth.

Ben looked back at her. "I would love to have a family and I'm ready, willing, and able."

Disturbed by his words, she rose and took Trey's bottle to the sink and washed it out. When she returned she chose to lean against the wall rather than sit back down. "Okay, so you're going to pick up Debra and drive her to the shopping center an hour before you're supposed to meet Norton. What about me and Trey? What do you want us to do?"

He grinned in amusement. "Oh, so we're through talking about me having a family, are we? Pity—I liked the subject."

"I don't think there's anything more to say. You answered my question."

"I'm always happy to oblige, Daisy. Whatever you want to know, whatever you want, you have only to ask."

And just like that the air between them could become charged. It was a situation unique in her experience. Ben fascinated her, and she found herself counting the hours remaining to them. "I'd like to know what you want me to do while you're meeting with Debra and her husband. Do you want me to stay here or go with you?"

His expression turned serious. "I need to know that you and Trey are absolutely safe, so I want you to stay here. I don't expect too much trouble, but I definitely don't want to take a chance."

She didn't like the idea that she wouldn't know what was happening. In fact, she didn't like any of the plan, especially the part about giving Trey back to his mother. And she *really* hated the part about not seeing Ben after that day, although she was having a little trouble figuring out exactly why.

watched, Campbell spoke into a device pinned to his lapel. "Norton is about to show up. Are you ready?"

Pale and resolute, Debra nodded. On impulse Ben reached out to her and covered her hand. "I know this is going to be hard for you to completely believe, Debra, but if you do exactly as I say, your husband will never be able to touch you again. Making that tape was brilliant and brave and it's going to give you a new life."

A tentative smile touched her lips. "Thank you, Ben. I hope you're right."

"I am." He glanced out the window, then gave her hand a reassuring squeeze. "He's here. Let's go."

Norton stood staring at the fountain as if lost in profound thought, with Campbell at his right, importantly guarding the other man's privacy. Norton's lean muscles had been honed to perfection by the best equipment and personal trainer money could buy, and Ben knew for a fact that his weak chin had been surgically enhanced to make him more photogenic. He had effectively packaged himself for the public. The problem was what was inside the package.

Norton turned quickly when he heard Ben speak his name and his gaze went straight to his wife. "Debra, thank goodness you're here! I've been so worried about you!"

"Really?" Debra said with cool composure. "How unusual."

Her response drew a frown from him. "You thought I *wouldn't* worry? Debra, I've been out of my mind with concern about you and Trey. Where is he, by the way?"

"He's somewhere safe."

He tried to take her hand, but she recoiled. "Don't touch me!"

Norton glanced around. "For God's sake, not so loud." He sliced a granite-hard look at Ben. "I guess I have you to thank for this."

"I'd be happy to accept the accolades, but Debra is the one who deserves them. She's finally had enough of you."

"I don't believe it. Debra—"

"Believe it, Peter. Believe it for all our sakes."

"But I love you and our son."

"We don't need your kind of love, Peter."

"I'll change."

"No, you won't." She pulled a videotape from her purse and held it out to him. "This is the second copy. The original and first copy are safe. You'll never know where they are."

He jerked it away from her. "*Campbell!* Take it out to the car and look at it. I want to know what's on it. And be quick about it!" He pasted a smile on his face for the benefit of two women who had recognized him and had stopped to look at him. Like the politician he aspired to be, he smiled at them. But his eyes were cold as his gaze returned to Ben. "You're going to pay for this. Debra's going to be sorry she ever heard your name."

"Oh, I see," Ben said with a calm designed to infuriate the other man. "So you don't care that you'll be completely ruined."

"You *son of a bitch*."

"Be careful, Peter," Debra said. "People are watching."

"If it's the last thing I do—"

"She's right, Norton. There's another group of shoppers over there who've stopped to look. Isn't it wonderful how popular and well thought of you are around here? I knew this would be a good place to meet."

Campbell came hurrying up to his employer, his expression anxious. "It's what McGuire said. It's you and Debra, and it's not good."

"Now do you understand?" Ben asked, his countenance stonelike. "If we release that tape, you'll be ruined, Norton. There won't be a man or woman left in Texas who will want to know you, and people all over America will be calling you a wife-beater and worse. Newspapers and television shows will do exposés revealing what a creep you are, and your political career will be over before it's even begun."

"You can't keep a man away from his son, McGuire!"

"I can and I will. And that's not all I can and will do. I'm going to stay in constant touch with Debra, and if you so much as phone her after we leave here today, much less try to see her, I'll take my copy of the videotape to the authorities, who will promptly throw your ass in jail. Tell me you understand."

Norton had lost all the color in his face and he was trembling with rage.

"*Tell* me, Norton," Ben said quietly.

"Damn you to hell, I *understand*."

NINE

Ben knew better than to trust Norton completely. He could visually identify all the men who had been in Norton's employ during his brief stint with the man, but Norton was perfectly capable of bringing in extra hired guns once he realized Debra had bolted, and probably had.

Consequently Ben took extra precautions to make sure he and Debra weren't followed, and he didn't go near the apartment until he was absolutely certain Norton hadn't put a tail on them. By the time he pulled into his parking space at the apartment, it was growing dark.

He opened the front door and saw Daisy. She was lying on a pallet on the living room floor with a happily babbling Trey beside her. The baby was playing with his blue horse, and she'd been singing to him. He knew she had been singing to Trey, because over the past few days he'd often seen her in the same situation, humming and singing to him, making up nonsensical lyrics about a baby boy named Trey and his blue horse and their wonderful magical adventures. For one unguarded moment he saw the softness of her expression, a result of her play time with Trey, but then in the next instant it changed to one of tension as she realized that Trey's mother was with him.

He ushered Debra in. "We're back, Daisy."

Slowly she got to her feet, bringing Trey with her.

As soon as Debra saw her son she rushed to him, her arms held out wide. "Trey!"

For a moment Daisy's grip tightened on the baby. Ben didn't think Debra noticed. Her attention was totally on her child as she reached for him. Then with an effort Ben was sure was visible only to him, Daisy released Trey to his mother.

Debra took her baby into her arms and held him as close to her as she could without hurting him. Tears of joy streamed down her face. "I've missed you so much, baby," she said, kissing the little boy.

Looking on, Daisy found it strangely hurtful to have to share the baby she had spent the past few days protecting and caring for. In fact, she found it almost intolerable. She wrapped her arms around herself and moved away from the two of them. "I gather everything went well?" she asked Ben, walking to him.

"Everything went fine." He leaned down and pressed a light kiss to her lips.

"What was that for?" she asked in surprise.

"For me. I missed you."

Emotion chased emotion through her too quickly for her to identify them. The fact that she was upset about losing Trey wasn't helping her reasoning power. She wasn't sure what Ben expected from her by way of a response. In the end she decided to simply go on to another subject. "What about Norton?"

"Once he sees that tape for himself, which I'm positive he has by now, he'll realize that getting his wife and son back is a lost cause. You don't get to be president of these United States by beating your wife."

"Norton for president? Now, there's a scary thought."

"I couldn't agree more."

Debra joined them with Trey in her arms and a huge smile on her face. "I would swear he has grown since I last saw him."

Daisy remained silent, so Ben spoke up. "Babies change fast at that age."

"I know, and I can't even begin to thank you two enough for taking such good care of him."

"As I told you over the phone, it was all Daisy's doing. She kept him out of the hands of the authorities and away from your husband's goons."

With her son cradled against her, Debra turned to Daisy. "I thanked you over the phone, but it's not enough. In fact, I don't think I'll ever be able to pay you back in any way, shape, or form for what you've done for Trey and me."

Daisy's gaze went to Trey. He was looking at her, his expression slightly perplexed, as if he didn't understand why she wasn't holding him. She couldn't stop herself from reaching out and caressing his small head. "No thanks are necessary. I'm just glad I'm the one who found him."

Debra wiped the tears from her face. "I am too."

Daisy knew it was stupid, but her arms felt strangely empty. She had had Trey only a matter of days, but she suddenly felt without purpose. She lifted her shoulders and let them fall. "You're a very brave woman."

"Not that brave. I should have done this a long time ago."

"So what are you going to do now?"

Debra looked at Ben for guidance, and he answered for her. "I'm going to drive Debra and Trey back to her motel tonight. I checked it out earlier today, and they'll be fine there. Then in the morning she can start out on her new life. Debra,

I assume you have a place in mind you want to settle."

She nodded. "I'm going back to the town where I grew up. It's a small town in Oklahoma, and my parents still live there."

Daisy gasped. "But won't that be dangerous? I mean, that'll be the first place your husband will think to look, wouldn't it?"

"You forget about the tape," Ben said. "That's her insurance."

"Besides," Debra said, "there's really no place I could go where he wouldn't find me if he tried. But as long as I've got the tape, he won't bother me. He's too smart for that."

Daisy looked at Trey, then back at Debra. "Well, it seems as if you've got everything figured out. I wish you the best of luck."

"Thank you."

"I'll get Trey's things together for you."

"I'll help," Ben said.

"That's not necessary," she said, already heading for the second bedroom, a foolish thought running through her mind. Debra's hair was short. Whose hair would Trey grab now? She fought back tears.

It was all ending, and she had the most incredible urge to be alone so that she could let her unshed tears flow. But it was not to be, at least not yet.

Ben followed her into the room and grasped her arm, bringing her to a halt. "I know how hard this is for you, honey, and I'm so sorry."

The small room offered no place for retreat, no place for privacy for her sorrow. "No, it's all right. Trey *should* be with his mother."

"Yes, he should, but that fact doesn't make it any easier on you."

"I'll be fine." She glanced around her. "I think his things are just about set to go." She waved a hand toward the bed and the boxes there. "His clothes and diapers are all folded and ready. His extra toys are packed too. His—"

"Daisy, look at me."

"What?"

"Look at me."

Until that moment she hadn't realized she had been avoiding his gaze. She lifted her head and searched his face. His mood was very somber, she realized. "Okay, I'm looking at you. What is it?"

"It'll take me an hour or so to get Debra to her motel and settled and then come back here. But when I return, you and I will finally have a chance to really talk about us."

"Us?" Surely there was nothing left to say. She certainly couldn't think of anything.

"Yes, Daisy, us. Since the beginning, we've had Trey with us along with the problem that surrounded him, but now it's about to be our turn."

He moved around her and gathered up the boxes. "I'll come back for his crib."

She nodded and waited until he had gone. She heard him telling Debra that he was going to load up the car and then he left by the front door. It was almost over. She drew a deep breath and walked back into the living room to gather Trey's toys from the floor.

She held out Trey's little blue horse and his set of disks to show Debra. "I bought these for him, and he really loves them. The disks just fit in his hand and he likes the sound he can make with them. Oh, and he sleeps with his blue horse. He likes it because it's so cuddly, and I've made up stories . . ." Her voice trailed off.

Debra nodded. "I'll be sure they stay within his reach. Thank you."

"Please stop thanking me. I couldn't have done any less than I did." Her voice sounded too sharp, she realized. Too sharp. She turned away. "I'll get his diaper bag. There's plenty of formula and cereal in there. You'll be fine for a few days."

When Daisy returned from the kitchen, Ben was heading out the door the second time, carrying the portable crib and baby seat. She set the diaper bag down beside Debra and looked at Trey. He favored his mother, she realized. They had the same blue-gray eyes, the same color hair.

"I was wondering—" She stopped and cleared

her throat. "I was wondering if you'd let me say good-bye to Trey."

Debra immediately stood and handed her son to Daisy. "Of course. I'll just wait in the car." She hesitated. "If you ever feel like driving up to Oklahoma, we'd love to see you. I'll be giving Ben my parents' address. You can always reach us through them."

"Thanks," Daisy said softly, stroking Trey's back. As soon as Debra left, Daisy walked to the rear of the apartment and stood by the back door. For a fleeting moment she wondered why she had done it, then decided that unconsciously she had wanted to get him as far away from his mother as was possible and have him all to herself one last time. Stupid of her, really. Stupid.

Tears stung her eyes and threatened to spill down her cheeks. Blinking them away, she pressed her face against Trey's and inhaled his baby scent for the last time. "I know you won't remember me," she whispered, "but I want you to know that there once was a lady who loved you very, very much." Trey softly cooed and reached out and grabbed a handful of her hair. "I expect you to be a good boy and grow up to be a fine man—okay?" Trey cooed again. They had carried on many conversations in just this manner. "I know you will. I do love you so. You're my sweet, sweet little boy."

"Daisy?" Ben said from behind her.

She tensed. "In a minute."

She heard his footsteps retreat to the living room. Sniffing back her tears, she shifted Trey in her arms so that she could see his face. "I'm going to send you a Christmas present every year, and I promise I'll come and see you." He gave her an angelic smile, just as if he'd understood every word she'd said, and she smiled back. "I love you, Trey." And one last time she hugged him to her. "Good-bye, sugar pie."

Then she took him into the living room and handed him to Ben.

Ben studied the moisture in her eyes with a frown. "Are you going to be all right, Daisy?"

"Of course I am."

"I'll hurry, I promise. I shouldn't be gone much more than an hour."

"I know. That's what you said a few minutes ago."

He hesitated. Her emerald eyes were awash with unshed tears. Her hair was disordered from Trey having grabbed it so often. She looked very beautiful and very sad. He longed to take her in his arms, to comfort her, and to tell her how much he loved her. But now was not the time. "I'll be back as soon as possible. Okay?"

"Okay."

But when he returned Daisy was gone.

———◈———◈———

After Ben left, Daisy gathered her things together and walked to the manager's apartment to use the phone to call a cab. Leaving wasn't exactly a conscious decision on her part as much as a basic need to get away from the place that without Ben and Trey seemed so terribly empty. It was as if in a few minutes all the life had left the place in which she had been so comfortable these past few days.

But if the apartment had seemed without life, her house seemed even more so. She didn't think she'd ever noticed before the lack of warmth in her house, the lack of coziness and homeyness. She had helped decorate many of her friends' homes, along with Caleb's, but now for the first time she realized that her own house lacked the loving and imaginative touches she had given the others. It didn't possess one plant or pet of any type. Ultimately it was just someplace she spent time between trips. In many ways she had felt more at home in the tiny apartment than she did in her own home.

But then, she had had Ben and Trey with her there. Here, in this sprawling two-story residence in one of the best sections of North Dallas, she was alone.

She turned on lights as she progressed through the downstairs rooms. She also made a point to stop in the den to turn on the radio. The rooms didn't seem quite so empty filled with music, and the chatter of the deejay between songs created the illusion that she wasn't as isolated as she felt.

On a corner table of the den the answering machine blinked annoyingly. Celeste had left a message, she remembered. That night in the club seemed so long ago, yet in reality it had been only days.

But if she needed a reminder that those days had been crammed to the brim with events, she didn't have to look farther than the back door through which she had entered. It had been forced open.

She punched the button on the answering machine and listened. The first message was from Celeste, telling her that two men had come into the bar, asking for her, and that Celeste was worried about her. She had talked to Celeste the next morning, she remembered. There were a couple of calls from Caleb, both from Algiers. He sounded happy and relaxed and in the mood to chat. On the second call he raised the possibility that she fly over and join him and Joy for the African safari they were thinking of taking the following week.

"I don't think so," she said aloud to the machine. Caleb was being thoughtful, but he and Joy deserved this time to themselves. Besides, she was in no mood to be sociable.

The remaining messages had been left by various friends, one with an invitation to a party for the coming weekend in California, one with news of a favorite rock band that would be coming to Austin soon and the rigors of the prospective ticket sales. Days ago she would have been happy to hear the news, but now the upcoming events elicited absolutely no interest.

After listening to all the messages, she reset the machine, then made one quick phone call to Celeste's home, hoping to get the answering machine. She didn't feel like facing Celeste's questions just yet.

She was in luck. At the beep she said, "Celeste, this is Daisy. I just wanted to let you know that I'm safe and sound and all is well. I'll talk to you in a few days. Bye."

Satisfied that she had alleviated any possible worries her friend might have been harboring since they had last spoken, she made her way upstairs to her bedroom where, on impulse, she started a fire in the fireplace.

She was tired, all her energies depleted, but she was too keyed up to sleep. A nice long bath, she decided, would be a welcome prescription. She stripped out of the jeans and T-shirt Ben had bought her and stepped into a hot bath filled with fragrant oils and bubbles.

Heaving a weary sigh, she leaned her head back against the bath pillow and closed her eyes. She hadn't realized how tense she'd been until gradually the heat of the water began to ease the tightness of her muscles. It felt good, she thought, letting her mind float free. . . .

A bath had been out of the question during the time she had cared for Trey. She had been too inexperienced with him to feel comfortable leaving him alone for any length of time. Lord, but she missed him terribly. What was he doing at this moment? Was it remotely possible he could be missing her. No, she thought. After all, he was only four months old. Besides he was probably asleep. Was his blue horse in the crib with him? She hoped so.

She had to stop thinking about him.

She had wanted a baby and for a little while had gotten one. But she had also gotten more than she had bargained for, because Ben had also been very much in the picture. For a few days she had lived her idea of a normal life. The three of them had been like an ordinary family, something she had never had. The only thing missing in her make-believe family had been a dog. They had had a plant, the cheerful little African violet. She hadn't brought it home with her because she hadn't wanted the reminder of a time that would never come again. Hopefully the next tenant would care for it and enjoy it.

But it didn't matter that her little family had been only imaginary, she forcefully reminded herself. After all, she had decided against just such a family. She wanted only a baby, unencumbered by a father.

Ben, she remembered, hadn't been at all enthusiastic about her plan. A small smile touched her lips. She supposed his attitude was understandable. In the overall scheme of things, most men considered themselves indispensable, and she had to admit that these last few days he had been just that—indispensable.

Of course, once most men were faced with the reality of the responsibility of a family, they ran, just as her father had.

Most men, she corrected herself. Not all.

Ben had stayed, but if she had asked him, would he have stayed beyond their few days together?

She lifted one arm out of the water and lazily scratched her nose. Was he back from taking Debra and Trey to their motel? Had he really returned to the apartment expecting to see her? By leaving she had saved them both the embarrassment of trying to think up a nice, painless way to say good-bye. Still, she couldn't help but wonder what he would think when he found that she had gone.

"You forgot something."

Her eyes flew open to see Ben, standing by the tub, the African violet in his hand.

Her hand flew to her breast. "You *scared* me!"

"I'd like to shake you," he said conversationally. He sat the African violet on the top of the commode and took a seat on its lid. "I rang the doorbell, but you didn't come to the door."

"I didn't hear it."

Making himself right at home, he leaned back against the tank and stretched his long legs out in front of him. "I figured as much. You've got the radio cranked up to earache volume."

"I wanted to be able to hear it up here." She inched lower in the tub until her chin touched the bubbled surface of the water. Silly, really, to be timid about her nudity since he had covered practically every inch of her skin with his mouth. But lounging there, his gaze a hard-eyed glint, he seemed a stranger. "So how did you get in?"

"The back door. The lock was broken. Norton's men, I assume?"

She nodded. "I think that's a safe assumption."

"I told you that you would be easy to find."

"I beg your pardon?"

"Your license plate. Remember? I told you I had copied down the number. Well, I traced it to get your address, just as they did."

"How clever. It's so nice to know that security is nothing more than an illusion."

"Unless you know what you're doing."

"Like you," she said crossly.

He nodded. "Like me."

For some reason she felt like throwing the wash-cloth at him. "Before you make yourself too comfortable, was there some reason in particular you wanted to see me?"

"Gee, Daisy, I don't know. Let me get a calculator so that I can count the reasons."

"There's no need to be sarcastic."

"There's every reason. Do you have any idea how I felt when I got back to the apartment and found you gone?"

A minute earlier, before she'd opened her eyes and seen him, she'd been wondering exactly that. "I hope you weren't worried."

"Actually I wasn't. I knew immediately what had happened. You'd bolted like a frightened deer."

"Excuse me, but I wasn't frightened. Why should I be frightened?"

"You tell me."

"I'm *not* frightened. Trey is safe, and all's well that ends well."

"Ends well? I don't see an ending, Daisy, not for you and me."

To give herself time to think, she fished beneath the water for the washcloth and rung it out. Finally she said, "I honestly think it's over, Ben."

"Well, you're wrong, because the truth is we haven't really gotten started yet."

She wasn't getting anywhere with him, and she felt at a decided disadvantage talking to him while she lay in the tub. "Okay, Ben. I'll tell you what.

If you would please wait in the other room, I'll get out and come in there and talk to you."

He straightened and rose to his feet. "I'll tell *you* what." He reached for a thick, fluffy towel. "I'll hold this towel for you while you get out and then we can go into the other room together."

"Oh, for goodness' sake, Ben! I'm not going to disappear down the drain if you leave me alone for two minutes."

"I'm sure you're right, nevertheless . . ." Without moving he opened the towel and held it out for her.

"Did anyone ever point out to you how stubborn you are?"

"Practically everyone I know."

Shaking her head, she rose and stepped out of the tub. He immediately wrapped the towel around her in the exact fashion she herself had used that first morning in his hotel when she had taken a shower in his suite. The sight of her wrapped in a towel, she remembered, had stopped him in his tracks. But now only the darkening of his gray eyes gave away that he was in any way affected as he tucked the towel between her breasts. She, however, couldn't say the same. The brush of his fingers against her skin produced an electrical jolt that ran straight through her.

"The bedroom, Daisy?"

It was a command, really, not a query. With a sigh she headed into the adjoining bedroom. But on her way out she snagged the cream cashmere bathrobe from the back of the door, shrugged into it, donned it, stripped off the towel, and belted the robe around her waist.

Feeling more properly clothed, she turned to Ben, who had again made himself comfortable, this time in an easy chair in front of the fire. To her consternation, she realized his masculinity was enhanced by the flowered chintz covering of the chair.

"Okay, Ben, this is the deal. We have just spent an intense few days together, and I think we can both agree that the intensity of what we were going through was a large factor in breeding what you might call an intimacy between us."

"Oh, come on, Daisy. *What you might call?*"

"The thing is, we both had plans before we met at X-S. Remember? You were going to Mexico to fish. I'm sure you have friends down there who are wondering what happened to you. As for me, I was planning to become a single parent. I still plan to do that—I just need a little time to choose a sperm bank. In the meantime, my cousin has asked me to join him and his wife for a safari in Africa, and I intend to go."

That was the first lie she had consciously told

him, but she felt she needed all the ammunition she could gather, especially since he might have been made of stone for all the reaction he was showing.

She cleared her throat. "I think the safari sounds like a lot of fun. Besides, the artificial insemination will take a while. But the main point I'm trying to make here is that we both should go on with our lives now. Your help was invaluable. I don't think that there's any question that together we did a really good thing. I think—"

"How much more of this do you have?" he asked quietly.

"Excuse me?"

"This malarkey. I'm getting tired of it."

"Ben—"

"In fact, I've just run out of patience. You don't believe what you're saying, so why should I?"

"That's not true."

"Yes, Daisy, it is. The question is, how can I make you realize it."

Her forehead creased. "Why would you even want to try?"

"Because I love you."

His admission stunned her and completely stole her breath. "Ben, you can't love me. You haven't known me that long."

He slowly smiled. "I understand what you're

saying, but apparently that fact doesn't make any difference."

She sank onto the end of the bed. When she had been younger, there had been boys who had told her they loved her. But as she had gotten older, the romantic stakes had naturally become higher. It was then that she had made the decision not to allow herself to get into the position where anyone's heart would be compromised, whether it was hers or the man's she was dating. Over the years her men friends had numbered high, but there had been no serious love interests. She'd been in control until then.

Ben had blindsided her.

"Daisy, I just told you I love you."

"I heard."

"You may not believe me," he said, his voice quiet, "but I've never told another woman I loved her."

"It's an extraordinary statement," she said slowly, "but I believe you. You wouldn't lie to me."

"So you know that, do you? You see? We may not have been together long, but we do know each other in ways people don't who have been together a hundred times longer than we have."

"I think I mentioned the intensity of our situation."

"Does it really matter *why*? In our case, isn't the result the important thing?"

She wasn't certain. She was still trying to deal with her shock. There was a very important fact here that wasn't lost on her: To tell a woman he loved her wouldn't be an idle or unimportant decision for a man like Ben.

Nothing had gone according to her plan since she had met him. Confusion and conflicting emotions had reigned, exactly as they were doing now.

She held out her hands, ultimately defeated by her attempt to come up with something clever or soothing to say. "Ben, I'm sorry, but I don't love you."

He was very still, very composed. Only a flicker of emotion in the depths of his eyes gave away that he was in any way disappointed. "I know that's what you think."

She shook her head. "No. It's what I know. Ben, I've tried to be as up front with you as I could. I told you that a father for my baby didn't figure into my plans. If I gave you the impression that there could be something more between us, I'm truly sorry. Beyond that I don't know what else to say."

"Fair enough. I certainly don't want you to say anything you'd regret later."

She wasn't so self-delusional that she thought she had handled the situation anywhere near approaching well, but she was totally taken by surprise when he pushed out of the chair, dropped down onto the bed beside her, and continued down with her until she was lying on her back and he was leaning over her.

"You say you don't love me—okay. But can you tell me you don't want me?" He smoothed her hair from her forehead with the palm of his hand. "Because, sweetheart, I sure as hell want you."

No, she thought. She couldn't tell him she didn't want him. Even now she could feel herself softening for him. His male scent and heat were sinking into her. She was amazed at herself and perturbed, but he didn't give her time to ponder her feelings. He trailed his fingers down to her lips, resting two of them on the fullness of her bottom lip and tugged until her lips parted.

He groaned softly. "Would you mind if I kissed you? Just once?"

"Yes . . . no . . . no . . ."

He lowered his head slowly, giving her time to hear the pounding of her own heartbeat in her ears. Time to feel the heat flood her veins and melt away her defenses. Time to object. It seemed a long time. . . .

He brought his mouth closer and closer to hers, and she didn't protest. Not when she began to feel his breath on her skin. Not when she felt that first touch of his lips against hers.

As if he were tentative and unsure of her reaction, he kissed her lightly, a mere brush of flesh against flesh. But that brush of his mouth created flames low in her belly, and she had the very sure feeling he knew exactly what he was doing.

The next kiss was more firm. It requested, it enticed nicely, sweetly, as if he were courting her with it. The kiss was a kind of beguilement and the worse kind of seduction because there was nothing to which she could object and there was everything she could enjoy. The sweetness mixed with the heat and drew her deeper beneath the spell of the moment—his spell.

With the next kiss came the persuasion. His tongue delved into her mouth, bringing to her his feel, his taste, and his real intent. But then, she already knew his intent: He wanted to make love to her. And she wanted it every bit as much as he did.

Outside, the night was deepening. Across the room the wood in the fire crackled and hissed. The music drifting up from the den had slowed down and was saturating the air with desire. At least that's what Daisy heard. And felt.

Desire seemed everywhere. It had soaked into her skin, her bones. It coated her hair; her hands and fingers were made of it, her veins were filled with it.

She slid her hands around his back. Through his shirt she felt the muscles shift and roll as he adjusted himself over her. She tightened her hold, bringing him closer, and his tongue plunged deep into her mouth with stark possession.

Her bathrobe had come open. Her breasts ached for his hand, her nipples throbbed for the feel of his lips. She twisted beneath him in silent supplication. And the kisses continued. . . .

Hot. Electric. Strong. Needful. Mind-blowing.

Then his hands began to explore and she couldn't keep the cry of satisfaction from her lips. Her hips, her stomach, her breasts, between her legs—his hand was everywhere. Fresh fires sprang up inside her until she felt completely engulfed.

With his lips and his hands Ben had completely taken over the control of her body. She was mindless with need for him.

She tore at his shirt, trying to undress him. She was desperate to feel his skin against hers, desperate to have him come inside her.

He was talking to her, but she couldn't understand what he was saying. He moved away from her. She grabbed out for him, but grasped nothing but air. A sob told of her disappointment. He murmured something to her, and then was back, pushing her robe from her shoulders, lifting her higher on the bed, covering her with his body, and finally, at last, driving into her.

He filled her, he thrilled her. She couldn't get enough of him. She grasped his hips and urged him deeper into her.

"Harder," she whispered. "Don't stop," she implored.

And he didn't. There was only passion and heat and most of all Ben. And she gave herself completely to him.

TEN

Leaving Ben sleeping soundly in her bed, Daisy quietly made her way downstairs the next morning and retrieved the newspaper from the front porch. She wasn't particularly eager to see what had gone on in the world in the past twenty-four hours, but she was determined to divert her mind from what had occurred between her and Ben during the night.

She sipped her coffee and stared blindly at the newspaper in front of her. She was disturbed. Deeply.

She had taken care not to wake Ben when she had gotten up because she had wanted this time alone to think, something she couldn't always do when he was near. Lines blurred and convictions faded when he was with her.

Last night their lovemaking had been entirely too consuming for her peace of mind, too electrifying. Something had been different and she was afraid she knew what it was. She had been more needful than she'd ever been with him before, too needful. In the midst of their passion she had given away vital parts of herself that now she regretted.

Consequently she felt bare and vulnerable, and she had made up her mind. As soon as Ben got up, she was going to ask him to leave. All she was waiting for was for him to come down so that she could tell him, and then she could get on with her life. The decision was a good one, an important one. She felt better having made the decision, and she was convinced that when he left she'd feel much more herself.

With an absent frown she sipped her coffee and stared at the paper. Little by little her eyes focused on the headline.

Norton Exposed.

A glance at the byline told her it was by the reporter Ben admired, Matthew Stone. She drew the paper closer, and she didn't have to read far to realize that Peter Norton's world had finally been systematically blown apart by the reporter.

The article cited names, times, and incidents that revealed Norton as a power-grubbing, paranoid egomaniac. It even listed a series of dirty tricks against opponents and showed big, wide trails that led straight to Norton with irrefutable proof backing his claims. The article even stated that Debra had taken their son and left.

Wow. Norton must be absolutely ballistic over this, she reflected wryly, and read on. As one of the examples of Norton's paranoia, the reporter named Ben, calling him elite, highly paid, and the best of the best in the world of security.

The best of the best. Another label.

She pondered the phrase, wondering what Ben would think of it. Since it was highly complimentary, she decided maybe he wouldn't mind. After a few more minutes of reading, she folded the paper and put it aside.

Now more than ever she was convinced that Debra and Trey would be all right. Quite simply Peter Norton was going to be too busy defending himself against Matthew Stone's article to think about his wife and son. And besides, he wouldn't want any more damaging evidence against him to come out. If he was clever enough, he might have a very slim chance to fight the words, but he would never be able to deny the video. Pictures spoke very loudly.

It seemed everything she had been involved with these past few days had been or soon would be resolved quite nicely. A vague pain twisted through her.

She turned her head and gazed out the window to the backyard. The most thought she'd ever given the backyard was when she wrote out the check to the young boy who mowed it. But a child needed a pleasant backyard to play in. Maybe she'd have a rose garden put in at the corner where her property abutted Caleb's. She could even start a vegetable garden. And eventually she could buy a swing set. . . .

If she went through with her plans to have a baby. If . . .

She wanted a child more than ever, but she was beginning to realize her initial decision to have one by artificial insemination had been a panicky one. First of all, she was too young for her biological clock to be going off. Besides, she now realized she had made the decision about having a baby when in effect she had been on the rebound from Caleb's marriage. She had missed him so much and had thought she could fill the hole his marriage had left in her life with a baby.

But now she wasn't certain that was a good enough reason anymore. When she finally decided to have a baby, she wanted it to be for the right reasons, for *unselfish* reasons that had more to do with bringing a new being into the world than filling up a hole in her life.

"Good morning," Ben said behind her, his voice deep and still rough from sleep.

Her nerves jumped. She looked up as he walked around the table and sat down across from her. "Good morning."

She treated herself to a lengthy look at him. His hair was wet from the shower and loosely combed into place. His face was freshly shaven, and when he had passed her on the way to the opposite chair, she had caught a whiff of spice cologne. His bare feet conjured an impression of casual intimacy in her mind. His jean-clad thighs conjured desire. She barely glanced at his white T-shirt, but instead lifted her gaze to his eyes, where lazy sexuality gleamed in the gray depths. "Ben—I want you to leave."

Amazingly a grin split his face. "Good morning? Ben, I want you to leave? Nice greeting, Daisy. Mind if I have some coffee first?" He reached for the pot and a spare cup.

Agitated, she smoothed the already-smooth tablecloth in front of her with her palm. "I'm sorry to be so abrupt. I know this must be unexpected."

His eyes glittered with both humor and steel, a combination she found to be extremely unsettling.

"Well, yes and no. No, because this isn't the first time you've made it known that you thought we should part. I'm sure it hasn't slipped your mind that just yesterday evening you walked out on me. I know it certainly hasn't slipped mine. And yes, it *is* unexpected. After last night I was hoping for something somewhat different."

"Like what?" Her fingers curled inward until her hand was a tight fist. "I mean, seriously, Ben— how much further do you really think we can go with this relationship?"

"As far as we want." The humor faded from his eyes, leaving only the steel. "Have you forgotten that I've fallen in love with you."

"I haven't forgotten, and I'm sorry, but—"

He held up his hand. "Stop right there. I don't really want to hear rationalizations or apologies. Daisy, I'll hate it like hell, but I'll leave if that's really what you want. The last thing I'd want to do is stay if it would make you miserable. But I'd like to know why."

She gazed at him blankly. "Why?"

"That's right. Tell me the *real* reason you're asking me to leave."

She nodded, trying to hurriedly regroup her thoughts. "Because I need to get on with my life."

"And remind me again why you can't get on with your life if I'm with you?"

"It would simply be too complicated."

"Too complicated? Why? Because your parents tried to split you apart with their divorce, and now you want a baby, but you don't want that baby to have a father in case the same thing happens again?"

She was confused to the point that she wasn't sure anymore if that was the real reason or not. But after a moment's hesitation she decided it was as good a reason as any to give Ben. "Yes, that's right."

"If a woman doesn't have a man in her life and she wants a baby, or if there's a health problem and she can't conceive, I don't see anything wrong with artificial insemination. But for you, Daisy, it's the wrong decision for the wrong reasons."

Her impulse was to completely disregard what he was saying, but something made her consider his words. "Why? Because you've said you love me?"

"Because it's wrong for me. And, yes, because I've told you I love you. I wish I could think of one hell of an argument that would convince you to love me, but I can't. Plain and simple, meeting you has changed my life. Because of my business, I've really never had a place I called home; I've always traveled and that suited me fine. There was no reason I needed to stay in one place. Then I met you and I knew immediately that I wanted you. Shortly after that I realized I was falling in love with you. And then there was Trey. He captured my heart too, but you never considered that, did you?"

She stared uncertainly at him. "It was obvious that you cared for him. You went to a lot of trouble."

"But you probably thought the trouble was for you or even for Debra. You think because your father left you that all men would be inclined to do the same thing. What about your cousin? Do you think if his wife has a baby, he'll up and leave them?"

"Absolutely not." The mere thought shocked her. Given the chance, Caleb would be a great father.

"Then would you at least consider the possibility that when I tell you I'd like nothing more than to marry you, settle down, and have children, and make a home that I'm telling you the truth?"

"M-marry me?" The idea of marriage was so foreign to her, she could barely get the words out.

"Yes, Daisy. I want to marry you and spend the rest of my life loving you. I can't make it any plainer than that."

Just for a moment the picture of a normal life flashed into her head, a picture of what it would be like if the scene they had lived out the past few days weren't make-believe and Trey would be replaced by a child that was a part of each of them.

But resistance toward the whole idea of what he was saying had been a part of her for so long, she couldn't let it go. "I can't marry you."

He studied her intently. "Are you sure, Daisy?"

"Yes." He was about to leave and she would be free, just as she wanted. And if her heart beat any faster, she would pass out. What was wrong with her?

"You know, it's funny. I've never been rejected by a woman before, and I've certainly never been rejected by a woman I love, because until you, I never loved. If I thought I could change your mind by badgering or arguing I would, but I don't. You're every bit as stubborn as I am, and I think it would be better if you reached the conclusion all by yourself that you love me."

"Ben, I'm not going to reach that conclusion."

"I hope you're wrong," he said quietly, a hint of pain glittering in his eyes. "I hope you're totally wrong. But in the meantime I'll leave. I just have to go up and finish dressing, then I'll get out of your way."

"But where will you go?"

His lips quirked. "I'm not homeless, Daisy. I have options."

"Like what?"

"Oh, I'll probably head down to Mexico for a while. It's a great place—you'd like it. I've got a whitewashed villa that sits on a bluff and overlooks the ocean. The waters are so blue there, sometimes I can't tell where the sky ends and the water begins." He paused. "As I said, you'd like it. I'll leave you that address so you'll know how to get in touch with me."

Her heart felt as if it were breaking, but that was

absurd. Everyone knew hearts didn't really break. Her lips firmed. "I won't need it."

"Nevertheless, you'll have it, along with another one. With that number you'll be able to reach me no matter where I am. But the first thing I'll do when I leave here this morning is drive over to the apartment and let the manager know we won't be back. And I still have some things there I need to pick up."

The apartment. Its image appeared in her mind. It was small and its furniture had seen better days, but it was cozy and comfortable and she wouldn't give anything for her time there. Of course it hadn't been the apartment that had made her stay so memorable, but the people with whom she had shared it. Now Trey was gone, and soon Ben would be too.

He stood and leaned over to press a soft kiss to her cheek.

"Good-bye, Daisy."

"Good-bye." She turned her head away from him and stared out the window until she heard him leave the room. She let out a long, shaky breath.

She felt as if she had been in a battle, but if she did, it had certainly been a battle of her own making. Ben had been very gentle with his arguments. He could have made it far worse on her, she realized, and she wouldn't have blamed him a bit.

She pictured him going upstairs to the bedroom where they had made such fabulous love during the night. He'd have to search to find his shoes and socks, she guessed. And there was no telling where his shirt was. But it probably wouldn't take him long and then he'd be gone, just as she had asked.

If there was one thing she had learned over the past few days, it was that a person should be extremely careful for what she wished. She had wished for a baby and had gotten Trey, only to have him taken away from her. She had wished that Ben would leave, and now he was doing just that.

Her nerves drew taut when a short time later she heard him come back down the stairs. She wasn't sure she could go through another farewell scene, but she needn't have worried. He left by the back door without ever saying another word to her.

And she found that she felt as empty and as without purpose as she had when she had handed Trey over to his mother. Only this time she felt worse, much worse.

For a long time she stared out at the backyard, thinking about a rose garden and a swing set and a child. But most of all she thought about Ben. And it was then, suddenly, that she realized she would never put in that rose garden and she'd never buy a swing set and she would certainly not have a child. At least not alone, not without Ben.

She was hopelessly in love with him.

The knowledge stunned her.

As she sat alone there at the table in her breakfast room, she went back over the past few days and had to conclude that the most surprising aspect of the realization was that she was surprised. She felt incredibly dumb. Why hadn't she seen it before? It seemed so obvious now.

Her only excuse was that the idea of being in love had scared her so much, she had spent most of her life carefully insulating herself from the emotion. And because she had, she had had to go on a stomach-churning roller-coaster ride of emotions before she could admit to herself that she was truly in love with Ben.

She lowered her head into her hands and groaned. He'd been right. She was stubborn and that was the nicest word she could think of to call herself.

But maybe she still had a chance.

She pushed out of the chair and headed for her purse. She had to get to the apartment before he left, and she didn't care if she broke every speed limit in the city doing it.

She grabbed her purse from the hall table, spun around, and found herself face-to-face with Peter Norton, Jr. She instantly recognized him from his photographs, but at first glance there seemed to be something not quite right about him. His eyes were glittering too brightly to be normal, his face was too flush. And he was pointing a gun at her.

"Where is he?"

"Who?"

"Your boyfriend, Ben McGuire. The bastard who convinced Debra to leave me."

"He didn't convince her. He didn't have to."

"Yes, he did," he hissed, small bubbles forming on his lips. "She would never have thought of it if he hadn't talked to her."

The man had mentally snapped, she realized, and the knowledge made his gun that much more frightening. "You're underestimating your wife, Mr. Norton."

He jammed the gun into her stomach. "*Don't* tell me what I'm doing. *Where is he?*"

The pressure of the gun's barrel against the soft flesh above her waist made it hard for her to breathe. "He's gone."

"Where?"

"I don't know."

He pushed the gun deeper, forcing her back against the hall table.

His breath smelled of liquor, his clothes were stained. His face was an evil leer. He was no longer a rational, balanced man. He had gone over the edge and crashed hard.

"You know. The only question is how bad am I

going to have to hurt you before you tell me. I want my wife and son back and I'll do anything necessary to get them."

She tried not to panic, but it was hard to maintain a façade of calm. "You can't bully me into telling you what I don't know. Besides, why do you want to know where he is? I heard him tell you that if anything happens to him, the tape will be made public."

His eyes grew huge with rage and the bubbles on his lips foamed bigger. "What the hell difference does it make now? I've got nothing else to lose. It's all gone. That damned reporter blew my life wide open this morning. I can't wait to take care of that son of a bitch." He pulled the gun up to the side of her neck and leaned into her. "You know what my damned public relations expert told me this morning after he'd seen Stone's hatchet job? The *same* damned public relations expert that I've paid over a million dollars to?"

She had no idea how to deal with him except try to humor him. "No, what?"

"He said no one would vote for a family man who no longer had a family because they had run from him in terror."

"He's got a point."

He slapped her with a hard backhand to her cheek. She gasped in pain and instinctively raised her hand to her face.

He grabbed her hand and twisted it behind her, and as he did he pressed his body against hers, close enough that she felt the pressure of his hard arousal against her lower body. His rough treatment and domination of her was exciting him, she realized. Nausea rose in her throat.

"I killed him and I'll do the same to that reporter *and* your boyfriend. And then I'm going after Debra and my son. Debra's nothing if not predictable. She'll go back to that no-nothing town she grew up in, and when she does, my men will grab her. No one takes my son from me. I'll get her back, and she'll pay."

Her stomach roiled, and she fought the nausea as fear for Debra and Trey rose in her. She had to start thinking clearly. This man couldn't be allowed to win, not after all Debra had gone through. And there was no way she would ever let him get his hands on Trey, not while she still drew a breath. She could only imagine the kind of man Trey would grow into if he were raised by his father. The idea was unbearable. And then there was Ben. Ben was smart and she knew he could take care of himself, but the thought that Norton might even lay a hand on him was intolerable.

Norton continued to talk to her, spewing out vile, loathsome things that seemed to excite him even more. The man was beyond reason.

Without giving herself too much time to think

about it, she brought up her knee with all the force she could muster, smashing it squarely between his legs.

He gave a grunt and folded over, his weight falling onto her. She gathered her strength and shoved the heel of her hand upward against his nose. With a piercing scream he staggered backward. The gun dropped from his hand and blood gushed from his nose.

She stared at him in shock. Over the years she'd taken a couple of self-defense courses, but she'd never been involved in a violent situation before, and she was momentarily fascinated by the damage she'd done to him. As she watched he straightened and looked at her, hate and insanity in his eyes. Icy fear encased her.

He charged her. "You *bitch*!"

Stunned, she wasn't fast enough to stop him from clamping his hands around her neck. Desperately she clutched at his wrists, trying to loosen his hold, but he was too strong for her. His hands tightened and tightened. She struggled to breathe. Her lungs began to hurt. She could feel the strength leave her body. Blackness began to descend. It closed around her. . . .

There was a distant sound, and then suddenly all pressure was released from her and she slumped to the floor.

She gasped for breath and clutched her throat.

She heard a loud thud. It sounded as if something had fallen, but at first she couldn't see what had made the noise. Her vision was blurred. She rubbed her eyes.

"Daisy, are you all right? God, talk to me! Say something."

It was Ben, she realized. Everything was going to be all right. She dropped her hands from her eyes and saw him standing over Norton, who lay crumpled in a heap on the floor.

"What are you doing here?" Her voice came out in a croak.

"I'll tell you later. Are you okay?"

She started to get up, but dizziness struck and she sank back down with a soft moan.

"Stay where you are." He grabbed her phone from the hall table and dialed 911. He gave the police all the pertinent facts, then knelt and felt for Norton's pulse.

"Is he dead?"

"No." With a grimace of displeasure he stood and came over to her. "He'll live to get his punishment. His money is going to be useless to help him out of this one." He dropped down beside her and lightly touched the red marks on her throat. "You're in pain, aren't you?"

"A little."

"Dammit, if I'd gotten here thirty seconds later . . ."

She attempted a grin. "No problem," she said hoarsely. "I had everything under control."

He gave a short laugh. "Yeah, right."

"Didn't you see the bloody nose I gave him?" It hurt to talk, but she was so happy to see him, she couldn't *not* talk to him.

"Yeah, baby, you did a great job. Lots of blood."

"Lots of blood," she repeated, not liking the way the memory of the blood was making her feel. She wet her dry lips. "By the way, what did you do to him? If he's not dead—"

He cast a careless glance over his shoulder. "He's unconscious. It's a move I learned long ago in another life."

"Will you teach it to me?" Her hand went back to her throat. In truth it hurt more than a little.

His smile held a wealth of tenderness she didn't feel she deserved. There was so much she wanted to tell him, but Norton lay three feet away and people would be arriving soon. And she wasn't feeling well. . . .

"I'll have to think about whether or not I want to teach you. I think nature armed you with enough weapons when you were born."

Her fingers rubbed up and down her neck. "Obviously not."

His eyes darkened with anger and pain. "I'm sorry, Daisy. I'm so damned sorry."

"It's not *your* fault."

"I shouldn't have let my personal feelings get in the way, but I did. I dropped my guard. It was totally unprofessional."

Sirens sounded in the distance.

"What do you mean?"

"I mean I was thinking only about you and the fact that you didn't love me."

"Oh, Lord, Ben, I—"

He shook his head. "No, don't talk now. I've got to deal with the police, and I want to make sure you get to the hospital."

The sirens drew closer and closer still.

"I'm not going to the hospital."

"Yes, Daisy, you are. Now, just stay there and I'll be right back."

The police arrived and for a little while it seemed to Daisy as if everyone were talking at once. She shut her eyes and tried to let the noise wash over her, but no matter how hard she tried, she could still hear Ben's voice.

She heard him explain to the police who he was and show some form of credentials and heard their voices turn to respect. He informed them that they weren't to question her until after she had been checked out by a doctor and they agreed. He explained to them in clear, concise terms the background that had led up to what had happened. Fortunately several had apparently read the morning paper and weren't as dubious about his report on Norton as they would otherwise have been.

Paramedics arrived and after a cursory examination put Daisy on a stretcher and took her to the hospital. By that time she was too tired to protest.

She awoke in her own bed, and the first thing she saw was Ben, asleep in an easy chair. His dark lashes formed sooty circles over his cheekbones. A night's growth of beard stubbled his face. Even though he was sleeping he looked tired, and she wondered when he had fallen asleep.

She remembered the bright lights and antiseptic smell of the hospital, but most of all she remembered Ben's worried face as he hovered over her. She remembered the doctor giving her something and telling her sleep would be the best thing for her. After that, nothing.

She stirred and he came instantly awake.

"What are you doing here?" Her voice came out in a raspy croak. She coughed and tried again. "You could have slept in another room." Her voice sounded better, just hoarse.

He straightened. "I preferred to keep an eye on you in case you needed something."

"That chair doesn't look too comfortable."

"I've slept in worse, believe me." His gaze was searching. "How are you?"

"Alive, thanks to you." She tried unsuccessfully to clear her throat. She opted for talking softly. "Norton?"

"He's locked up and hopefully that's how he'll stay for a long time. He's being charged not only with assault on Debra, but the murder of his public relations expert and the attempted murder of you as well. He could have been let out on bail, but the judge was tough." He grinned. "I have some contacts down at the jail where Norton was being arraigned and I arranged for the judge to see the tape. Norton's lawyer had to work to get his client special consideration, but he had two things going for him. There was no doubt that Norton would be a high-profile security risk and there was equally no doubt that his client is as crazy as a loon. The judge agreed to have him held in a secured section of the hospital until a psychiatric workup is completed. After that he will be brought before the judge again, but all three cases against Norton are excellent. He's guilty as sin, as we well know."

She pushed herself upward. Ben sprang to help her, arranging pillows behind her, then he eased down on the bed at her side and took her hand. "What can I get you? Tea and honey might be a good thing to start off with."

"In a minute. For now just water." She sipped the water he handed her. "Ben, why did you come back?"

"I stopped at a newsstand to get a paper and saw Stone's article. The minute I read it I knew there'd be trouble."

"That's more than I knew. I read it and didn't think too much about it except to be glad that Norton had finally been exposed."

He shook his head, his face grim. "I should have anticipated trouble—Stone had been getting closer and closer. But as I told you yesterday, I've been letting my personal feelings get in the way of my professional judgment, and I made a serious error."

"Don't criticize yourself, Ben. You've been wonderful."

He looked at her oddly. "Do you mean that?"

"Absolutely." She took another drink of water, then put the glass on the nightstand beside the bed.

Using his fingers, he lightly combed curling tendrils of her hair off her face. "I'm glad you think so, but I'm not sure how much longer you're going to hold that opinion. I've got something to tell you." His expression was bleak and his eyes darkened as he touched the bruises on her throat. "I know I said I'd leave, but I don't think I can, not without you."

"Ben—"

"No, don't talk, just listen. I've been thinking about this. You were right when you said everything had happened too fast. And it's all my fault. In the job I've done for most of my adult life, emotions are a distinct liability. I was trained to suppress them, and as I said once before, I was very good. And fortunately or unfortunately—however you want to look at it—practices and tendencies from my previous job have carried over to the present."

"Ben—"

"Shhh. Listen." His fingers gently stroked the dark smudges on her neck. "Then I met you and a funny thing happened. Suddenly I couldn't suppress my emotions any longer. In fact, they all came out at once. They overwhelmed me and they overwhelmed you. That was a mistake. I should have known better than to let that happen."

"Ben—"

"Come to Mexico with me, Daisy. You can recuperate down there. I won't make any demands on you. I just want to be with you, give you time to get over this, and then maybe—"

"*Ben!*" Her raised voice got his attention, but the strain on her voice caused her to cough. When she stopped she lowered her voice again and spoke softly. "Will you please listen to me now?"

He eyed her warily. "Okay, what is it?"

"I was on my way to try to intercept you at the apartment, when Norton stopped me. I wanted to tell you how blind I'd been. How stupid. Ben—I wanted to tell you I loved you."

Lines formed in his forehead, and a faint light of hope appeared in his eyes. "Are you sure? I mean, you've been through a lot."

"Oh, I'm sure, I'm *definitely* sure. I've never been more sure of anything in my life. And I'd love to go to Mexico. In fact, try and stop me from going."

With an exclamation he gathered her tenderly in his arms and simply held her. "God, Daisy, to think I almost lost you."

"You wouldn't have lost me," she whispered. "Fate wouldn't have been that cruel."

"No?"

"No."

A shudder of relief and happiness shook him. "When we get to Mexico, we can start working on making a baby."

She pulled away, gazed up at him, and lovingly caressed his face. "Why wait?"

THE EDITOR'S CORNER

Since the inception of LOVESWEPT in 1983, we've been known as the most innovative publisher of category romance. We were the first to publish authors under their real names and show their photographs in the books. We originated interconnected "series" books and established theme months. And now, after publishing over 700 books, we are once again changing the face of category romance.

Starting next month, we are introducing a brand-new LOVESWEPT look. We're sure you'll agree with us that it's distinctive and outstanding—nothing less than the perfect showcase for your favorite authors and the wonderful stories they write.

A second change is that we are now publishing four LOVESWEPTs a month instead of six. With so many romances on the market today, we want to provide you with only the very best in romantic fiction. We know that you want quality, not quantity, and we are as committed as ever to giving you love stories you'll never forget, by authors you'll always remember. We are especially proud to debut our new look with four sizzling romances from four of our most talented authors.

Starting off our new look is Mary Kay McComas with **WAIT FOR ME**, LOVESWEPT #702. Oliver Carey saves Holly Loftin's life during an earthquake with a split-second tackle, but only when their eyes meet does he feel the earth tremble and her compassionate soul reach out to his. He is intrigued by her need to help others, enchanted by her appetite for simple pleasures, but now he has to show her that their differences can be their strengths and that, more than anything, they belong together. Mary Kay will have you laughing and crying with this touching romance.

The ever-popular Kay Hooper is back with her unique blend of romantic mystery and spicy wit in **THE HAUNTING OF JOSIE**, LOVESWEPT #703. Josie Douglas decides that Marc Westbrook, her gorgeous landlord, would have made a good warlock, with his raven-dark hair, silver eyes, and even a black cat in his arms! She chose the isolated house as a refuge, a place to put the past to rest, but now Marc insists on fighting her demons . . . and why does he so resemble the ghostly figure who beckons to her from the head of the stairs? Kay once more demonstrates her talent for seduction and suspense in this wonderful romance.

Theresa Gladden proves that opposites attract in **PERFECT TIMING**, LOVESWEPT #704. Jenny Johnson isn't looking for a new husband, no matter how many hunks her sister sends her way, but Carter Dalton's cobalt-blue eyes mesmerize her into letting his daughter join her girls' club—and inviting him to dinner! The free-spirited rebel is all wrong for him: messy house, too many pets, wildly disorganized—but he can't resist a woman who promises to fill the empty spaces he didn't know he had. Theresa's spectacular romance will leave you breathless.

Last but certainly not least is **TAMING THE PIRATE**, LOVESWEPT #705, from the supertalented Ruth Owen. When investigator Gabe Ramirez sees Laurie Palmer, she stirs to life the appetites of his buccaneer ancestors and makes him long for the golden lure of her smile. She longs to trade her secrets for one kiss from his brigand's lips, but once he knows why she is on the run, will he betray the woman he's vowed will never escape his arms? You won't forget this wonderful story from Ruth.

Happy reading,

With warmest wishes,

Nita Taublib

Nita Taublib
Deputy Publisher

P.S. Don't miss the exciting women's novels from Bantam that are coming your way in August—**MIDNIGHT WARRIOR**, by *New York Times* bestselling author Iris Johansen, is a spellbinding tale of pursuit, possession, and passion that extends from the wilds of Normandy to untamed medieval England; **BLUE MOON** is a powerful and romantic novel of love and families by the exceptionally talented Luanne Rice. *The New York Times Book Review* calls it "a rare combination of realism and romance"; **VELVET**, by Jane Feather, is a spectacular novel of danger and deception in which a beautiful woman risks all for revenge and love; **THE WITCH DANCE**, by Peggy Webb, is a poignant story of two lovers whose passion breaks every rule. We'll be giving you a sneak peek at these terrific books in next month's LOVESWEPTs. And immediately following this page, look for a preview of the exciting romances from Bantam that are *available now!*

Don't miss these extraordinary books by
your favorite Bantam authors

On sale in June:

MISTRESS
by Amanda Quick

WILDEST DREAMS
by Rosanne Bittner

DANGEROUS TO LOVE
by Elizabeth Thornton

AMAZON LILY
by Theresa Weir

"One of the hottest and most prolific writers in romance today."
—*USA Today*

MISTRESS
Available in hardcover
by the *New York Times*
bestselling author

AMANDA QUICK

With stories rife with wicked humor, daring intrigue, and heart-stopping passion, Amanda Quick has become a writer unmatched in the field of romantic fiction. Now the author of fourteen New York Times *bestselling novels offers another unforgettable tale as a proper spinster embarks on a delicious masquerade and a handsome earl finds himself tangling with the most exotic and captivating mistress London has ever known.*

"Power, passion, tragedy, and triumph
are Rosanne Bittner's hallmarks. Again and
again, she brings readers to tears."
—*Romantic Times*

WILDEST DREAMS
by

ROSANNE
BITTNER

Against the glorious panorama of big sky country, award-winning Rosanne Bittner creates a sweeping saga of passion, excitement, and danger ... as a beautiful young woman and a rugged ex-soldier struggle against all odds to carve out an empire—and to forge a magnificent love.

Here is a look at this powerful novel ...

Lettie walked ahead of him into the shack, swallowing back an urge to retch. She gazed around the cabin, noticed a few cracks between the boards that were sure to let in cold drafts in the winter. A rat scurried across the floor, and she stepped back. The room was very small, perhaps fifteen feet square, with a potbellied stove in one corner, a few shelves built against one wall, and a crudely built table in the middle of the room, with two crates to serve as chairs. The bed was made from pine, with ropes for springs and no mattress on top. She was glad her mother had given her two feather mattresses before they parted. Never had she longed more fervently to be with her family back at the spacious home they had left behind in St.

Joseph, where people lived in reasonable numbers, and anything they needed was close at hand.

Silently, she untied and removed the wool hat she'd been wearing. She was shaken by her sense of doubt, not only over her choice to come to this lonely, desolate place, but also over her decision to marry. She loved Luke, and he had been attentive and caring and protective throughout their dangerous, trying journey to get here; but being his wife meant fulfilling other needs he had not yet demanded of her. This was the very first time they had been truly alone since marrying at Fort Laramie. When Luke had slept in the wagon with her, he had only held her. Was he waiting for her to make the first move; or had he patiently been waiting for this moment, when he had her alone? Between the realization that he would surely expect to consummate their marriage now, and the knowledge that she would spend the rest of the winter holed up in this tiny cabin, with rats running over her feet, she felt panic building.

"Lettie?"

She was startled by the touch of Luke's hand on her shoulder. She gasped and turned to look up at him, her eyes wide with fear and apprehension. "I . . . I don't know if I can stay here, Luke." Oh, why had she said that? She could see the hurt in his eyes. He should be angry. Maybe he would throw her down and have his way with her now, order her to submit to her husband, yell at her for being weak and selfish, tell her she would stay here whether she liked it or not.

He turned, looked around the tiny room, looked back at her with a smile of resignation on his face. "I can't blame you there. I don't know why I even considered this. I guess in all my excitement . . ." He sighed deeply. "I'll take you back to Billings in the morning. It's not much of a town, but maybe I can find a safe place for you and Nathan to stay while I make things more livable around here."

"But . . . you'd be out here all alone."

He shrugged, walking over to the stove and opening the door. "I knew before I ever came here there would be a lot of lonely living I'd have to put up with." He picked up some kindling from a small pile that lay near the stove and stacked it inside. "When you have a dream, you simply do what you have to do to realize it." He turned to face her. "I told you it won't be like this forever, Lettie, and it won't."

His eyes moved over her, and she knew what he wanted. He simply loved and respected her too much to ask for it. A wave of guilt rushed through her, and she felt like crying. "I'm sorry, Luke. I've disappointed you in so many ways already."

He frowned, coming closer. "I never said that. I don't blame you for not wanting to stay here. I'll take you back to town and you can come back here in the spring." He placed his hands on her shoulders. "I love you, Lettie. I never want you to be unhappy or wish you had never married me. I made you some promises, and I intend to keep them."

A lump seemed to rise in her throat. "You'd really take me to Billings? You wouldn't be angry about it?"

Luke studied her face. He wanted her so, but was not sure how to approach the situation because of what she had been through. He knew there was a part of her that wanted him that way, but he had not seen it in her eyes since leaving Fort Laramie. He had only seen doubt and fear. "I told you I'd take you. I wouldn't be angry."

She suddenly smiled, although there were tears in her eyes. "That's all I need to know. I . . . I thought you took it for granted, just because I was your wife . . . that you'd demand . . ."

She threw her arms around him, resting her face against his thick fur jacket. "Oh, Luke, forgive me. You don't have to take me back. As long as I know I *can* go back, that's all I need to know. Does that make any sense?"

He grinned. "I think so."

Somewhere in the distance they heard the cry of a bobcat. Combined with the groaning mountain wind, the sounds only accentuated how alone they really were, a good five miles from the only town, and no sign of civilization for hundreds of miles beyond that. "I can't let you stay out here alone. You're my husband. I belong here with you," Lettie said, still clinging to him.

Luke kissed her hair, her cheek. She found herself turning to meet his lips, and he explored her mouth savagely then. She felt lost in his powerful hold, buried in the fur jacket, suddenly weak. How well he fit this land, so tall and strong and rugged and determined. She loved him all the more for it.

He left her mouth, kissed her neck. "I'd better get a fire going, bring in—"

"Luke." She felt her heart racing as all her fears began to melt away. She didn't know how to tell him, what to do. She could only look into those handsome blue eyes and say his name. She met his lips again, astonished at the sudden hunger in her soul. How could she have considered letting this poor man stay out here alone, when he had a wife and child who could help him, love him? And how could she keep denying him the one thing he had every right to take for himself? Most of all, how could she deny her own sudden desires, this surprising awakening of woman that ached to be set free?

"Luke," she whispered. "I want to be your wife, Luke, in every way. I want to be one with you and know that it's all right. I don't want to be afraid any more."

DANGEROUS TO LOVE
by Elizabeth Thornton

"A major, major talent . . . a genre superstar."
—*Rave Reviews*

Dangerous. Wild. Reckless. Those were the words that passed through Serena Ward's mind the moment Julian Raynor entered the gaming hall. If anyone could penetrate Serena's disguise—and jeopardize the political fugitives she was delivering to freedom—surely it would be London's most notorious gamester. Yet when the militia storms the establishment in search of traitors, Raynor provides just the pretext Serena needs to escape. But Serena is playing with fire . . . and before the night is through she will find herself surrendering to the heat of unsuspected desires.

The following is a sneak preview of what transpires that evening in a private room above the gaming hall. . .

"Let's start over, shall we?" said Julian. He returned to the chair he had vacated. "And this time, I shall try to keep myself well in check. No, don't move. I rather like you kneeling at my feet in an attitude of submission."

He raised his wine glass and imbibed slowly. "Now you," he said. When she made to take it from him, he shook his head. "No, I shall hold it. Come closer."

Once again she found herself between his thighs. She didn't know what to do with her hands, but he knew.

"Place them on my thighs," he said, and Serena obeyed. Beneath her fingers, she could feel the hard masculine muscles bunch and strain. She was also acutely aware of the movements of the militia as they combed the building for Jacobites.

"Drink," he said, holding the rim of the glass to her lips, tipping it slightly.

Wine flooded her mouth and spilled over. Choking, she swallowed it.

"Allow me," he murmured. As one hand cupped her neck, his head descended and his tongue plunged into her mouth.

Shock held her rigid as his tongue thrust, and thrust again, circling, licking at the dregs of wine in her mouth, lapping it up with avid enjoyment. When she began to struggle, his powerful thighs tightened against her, holding her effortlessly. Her hands went to his chest to push him away, and slipped between the parted edges of his shirt. Warm masculine flesh quivered beneath the pads of her fingertips. Splaying her hands wide, with every ounce of strength, she shoved at him, trying to free herself.

He released her so abruptly that she tumbled to the floor. Scrambling away from him, she came up on her knees. They were both breathing heavily.

Frowning, he rose to his feet and came to tower over her. "What game are you playing now?"

"No game," she quickly got out. "You are going too fast for me." She carefully rose to her feet and began to inch away from him. "We have yet to settle on my . . . my remuneration."

"Remuneration?" He laughed softly. "Sweetheart, I have already made up my mind that for a woman of your unquestionable talents, no price is too high."

These were not the words that Serena wanted to hear, nor did she believe him. Men did not like greedy women. Although she wasn't supposed to know it, long before his marriage, her brother, Jeremy, had given his mistress her *congé* because the girl was too demanding. What was it the girl had wanted?

Her back came up against the door to the bedchamber. One hand curved around the door-knob in a reflexive movement, the other clutched the door-jamb for support.

Licking her lips, she said, "I . . . I shall want my own house."

He cocked his head to one side. As though musing to himself, he said, "I've never had a woman in my keeping. Do you know, for the first time, I can see the merit in it? Fine, you shall have your house."

He took a step closer, and she flattened herself against the door. "And . . . and my own carriage?" She could hardly breathe with him standing so close to her.

"Done." His eyes were glittering.

When he lunged for her, she cried out and flung herself into the bed-chamber, slamming the door quickly, bracing her shoulder against it as her fingers fumbled for the key.

One kick sent both door and Serena hurtling back. He stood framed in the doorway, the light behind him, and every sensible thought went out of her head. Dangerous. Reckless. Wild. This was all a game to him!

He feinted to the left, and she made a dash for the door, twisting away as his hands reached for her. His fingers caught on the back of her gown, ripping it to the waist. One hand curved around her arm, sending her sprawling against the bed.

There was no candle in the bed-chamber, but the lights from the tavern's courtyard filtered through the window casting a luminous glow. He was shedding the last of his clothes. Although everything in her revolted against it, she knew that the time had come to reveal her name.

Summoning the remnants of her dignity, she said, "You should know that I am no common doxy. I am a high-born lady."

He laughed in that way of his that she was coming to thoroughly detest. "I know," he said, "and I am to play the conqueror. Sweetheart, those games are all very well in their place. But the time for games is over. I want a real woman in my arms tonight, a willing one and not some character from a fantasy."

She turned his words over in her mind and

could make no sense of them. Seriously doubting the man's sanity, she cried out, "Touch me and you will regret it to your dying day. Don't you understand anything? I am a lady. I . . ."

He fell on her and rolled with her on the bed. Subduing her easily with the press of his body, he rose above her. "Have done with your games. I am Julian. You are Victoria. I am your protector. You are my mistress. Yield to me, sweeting."

Bought and paid for—that was what was in his mind. She was aware of something else. He didn't want to hurt or humiliate her. He wanted to have his way with her. He thought he had that right.

He wasn't moving, or forcing his caresses on her. He was simply holding her, watching her with an unfathomable expression. "Julian," she whispered, giving him his name in an attempt to soften him. "Victoria Noble is not my real name."

"I didn't think it was," he said, and kissed her.

His mouth was gentle; his tongue caressing, slipping between her teeth, not deeply, not threateningly, but inviting her to participate in the kiss. For a moment, curiosity held her spellbound. She had never been kissed like this before. It was like sinking into a bath of spiced wine. It was sweet and intoxicating, just like the taste of him.

Shivering, she pulled out of the embrace and stared up at him. His brows were raised, questioning her. All she need do was tell him her name and he would let her go.

Suddenly it was the last thing she wanted to do.

An All-Time Recommended Read in the
Romance Reader's Handbook

AMAZON LILY

by the spectacular

Theresa Weir

"Theresa Weir's writing is poignant,
passionate and powerful . . . will capture the
hearts of readers."—*New York Times*
bestselling author Jayne Ann Krentz

Winner of Romantic Times *New Adventure Writer
Award, Theresa Weir captures your heart with this truly
irresistible story of two remarkable people who must battle
terrifying danger even as they discover breathtaking love.*
Rave Reviews *had praised it as "a splendid adventure . . .
the perfect way to get away from it all,"* and Rendezvous
insists that you "put it on your must-read list."

"You must be the Lily-Libber who's going to San
Reys."

The deep voice that came slicing through Corey's
sleep-fogged brain was gravelly and rough-edged.

She dragged open heavy-lidded eyes to find herself
contemplating a ragged pair of grubby blue tennis
shoes. She allowed her gaze to pan slowly northward,
leaving freeze-framed images etched in her mind's
eye: long jeans faded to almost white except along the
stitching; a copper waistband button with moldy let-
tering; a large expanse of chest-filled, sweat-soaked
T-shirt; a stubbly field of several days growth of whisk-
ers; dark aviator sunglasses that met the dusty, sweaty
brim of a New York Yankees baseball cap.

Corey's head was bent back at an uncomfortable angle. Of course, Santarém, Brazil, wasn't Illinois, and this person certainly wasn't like any case she'd ever handled in her job as a social worker.

The squalid air-taxi building was really little more than a shed, and it had been crowded before, with just Corey and the files. But now, with this man in front of her giving off his angry aura . . . She couldn't see his eyes, but she could read enough of his expression to know that she was being regarded as a lower form of life or something he might have scraped off the bottom off his shoe.

She knew she wasn't an American beauty. Her skin was too pale, her brown eyes too large for her small face, giving her a fragile, old-world appearance that was a burden in these modern times. People had a tendency to either overlook her completely or coddle her. But his reaction was something totally new.

The man's attention shifted from her to the smashed red packet in his hand. He pulled out a flattened nonfilter cigarette, smoothed it until it was somewhat round, then stuck it in the corner of his mouth. One hand moved across the front of the faded green T-shirt that clung damply to his corded muscles. He slapped at the breast pocket. Not finding what he was searching for, both of his hands moved to the front pockets of the ancient jeans that covered those long, athletic legs. There was a frayed white horizontal rip across his right knee, tan skin and sun-bleached hair showing through. Change jingled as he rummaged around to finally pull out a damp, wadded-up book of matches.

"Damn," he muttered after the third match failed to light. "Gotta quit sweating so much." He tossed the bedraggled matchbook to the floor. Cigarette still in his mouth, his hands began a repeat search of his pockets.

Corey reached over to where her twill shoulder bag was lying on a stack of tattered *Mad* magazines. She unzipped a side pocket and pulled out the glossy black and gold matches she'd been saving to add to her matchbook collection.

He grabbed them without so much as a thank-you. "That's right—" he said, striking a match, "you girl scouts are always prepared." He shook out the match and tossed it to the floor.

"Are you Mike Jones?" She hoped to God he wasn't the pilot she was waiting for.

"No." He inhaled deeply, then exhaled, blowing a thick cloud of smoke her direction.

"Do you know when Mr. Jones will be here?" she asked, willing her eyes not to bat against the smoke.

"*Mister* Jones had a slight setback. He was unconscious last time I saw him." The man read the ornate advertisement for the Black Tie restaurant on the match cover, then tucked the matches into the breast pocket of his T-shirt. The knuckles of his hand were red and swollen, one finger joint cracked and covered with dried blood.

"I found Jones in a local cantina, drunk out of his mind and just itching to fly. Had a little trouble convincing him it would be in his best interest if he stayed on the ground. My name's Ash—Asher Adams, and it looks like I'll be flying you to the reserve. If you still want to go."

Corey pushed her earlier thoughts to the back of her mind. "Of course I still want to go." She hadn't come this far to back out now.

"You want my advice?" He pulled off the navy-blue cap and swiped at his sweating forehead before slapping the cap back over shaggy brown hair. "Go back home. Get married. Have babies. Why is it you women have to prove you're men? You come here thrill-seeking so you can go home and be some kind of small-town hero. So your whole puny story can be printed up in a little four-page county paper and you can travel around to all the local clubs and organizations with your slide presentation, and all your friends can ooh and aah over you."

Corey felt heated anger flushing her face. She pressed her lips together in a firm, stubborn line.

What an obnoxious boor! In her years as a social worker, she'd never, *never* come across anyone like him. And thank God for that, she fumed.

Asher Adams took another drag off his cigarette, then flopped down in the chair across from her, legs sticking out in front of him, crossed at the ankles. "Go back home," he said in a weary voice. "This is real. It isn't some Humphrey Bogart movie. This isn't Sleepyville, Iowa, or wherever the hell you're from—"

"Pleasant Grove, Illinois," she flatly informed him. "And I don't need your advice. I don't want it." Who did this overbearing man think he was? She hadn't taken vacation time to come here and be insulted by an ill-tempered woman-hater. And he talked as if she planned to settle in the jungles of Brazil. There was nothing further from her mind.

She zipped her bag and grabbed up her cream-colored wool jacket. "I'd like to leave now."

And don't miss these fabulous romances from Bantam Books, on sale in July:

MIDNIGHT WARRIOR
by the *New York Times* bestselling author
Iris Johansen
"Iris Johansen is a master among master stoytellers."
—*Affaire de Coeur*

BLUE MOON
by the nationally bestselling author
Luanne Rice
"Luanne Rice proves herself a nimble virtuoso."
—*The Washington Post Book World*

VELVET
by the highly acclaimed
Jane Feather
"An author to treasure."
—*Romantic Times*

THE WITCH DANCE
by the incomparable
Peggy Webb
"Ms. Webb has an inventive mind brimming with originality that makes all of her books special reading."
—*Romantic Times*

OFFICIAL RULES

To enter the sweepstakes below carefully follow all instructions found elsewhere in this offer.

The **Winners Classic** will award prizes with the following approximate maximum values: 1 Grand Prize: $26,500 (or $25,000 cash alternate); 1 First Prize: $3,000; 5 Second Prizes: $400 each; 35 Third Prizes: $100 each; 1,000 Fourth Prizes: $7.50 each. Total maximum retail value of Winners Classic Sweepstakes is $42,500. Some presentations of this sweepstakes may contain individual entry numbers corresponding to one or more of the aforementioned prize levels. To determine the Winners, individual entry numbers will first be compared with the winning numbers preselected by computer. For winning numbers not returned, prizes will be awarded in random drawings from among all eligible entries received. Prize choices may be offered at various levels. If a winner chooses an automobile prize, all license and registration fees, taxes, destination charges and, other expenses not offered herein are the responsibility of the winner. If a winner chooses a trip, travel must be complete within one year from the time the prize is awarded. Minors must be accompanied by an adult. Travel companion(s) must also sign release of liability. Trips are subject to space and departure availability. Certain black-out dates may apply.

The following applies to the sweepstakes named above:

No purchase necessary. You can also enter the sweepstakes by sending your name and address to: P.O. Box 508, Gibbstown, N.J. 08027. Mail each entry separately. Sweepstakes begins 6/1/93. Entries must be received by 12/30/94. Not responsible for lost, late, damaged, misdirected, illegible or postage due mail. Mechanically reproduced entries are not eligible. All entries become property of the sponsor and will not be returned.

Prize Selection/Validations: Selection of winners will be conducted no later than 5:00 PM on January 28, 1995, by an independent judging organization whose decisions are final. Random drawings will be held at 1211 Avenue of the Americas, New York, N.Y. 10036. Entrants need not be present to win. Odds of winning are determined by total number of entries received. Circulation of this sweepstakes is estimated not to exceed 200 million. All prizes are guaranteed to be awarded and delivered to winners. Winners will be notified by mail and may be required to complete an affidavit of eligibility and release of liability which must be returned within 14 days of date on notification or alternate winners will be selected in a random drawing. Any prize notification letter or any prize returned to a participating sponsor, Bantam Doubleday Dell Publishing Group, Inc., its participating divisions or subsidiaries, or the independent judging organization as undeliverable will be awarded to an alternate winner. Prizes are not transferable. No substitution for prizes except as offered or as may be necessary due to unavailability, in which case a prize of equal or greater value will be awarded. Prizes will be awarded approximately 90 days after the drawing. All taxes are the sole responsibility of the winners. Entry constitutes permission (except where prohibited by law) to use winners' names, hometowns, and likenesses for publicity purposes without further or other compensation. Prizes won by minors will be awarded in the name of parent or legal guardian.

Participation: Sweepstakes open to residents of the United States and Canada, except for the province of Quebec. Sweepstakes sponsored by Bantam Doubleday Dell Publishing Group, Inc., (BDD), 1540 Broadway, New York, NY 10036. Versions of this sweepstakes with different graphics and prize choices will be offered in conjunction with various solicitations or promotions by different subsidiaries and divisions of BDD. Where applicable, winners will have their choice of any prize offered at level won. Employees of BDD, its divisions, subsidiaries, advertising agencies, independent judging organization, and their immediate family members are not eligible.

Canadian residents, in order to win, must first correctly answer a time limited arithmetical skill testing question. Void in Puerto Rico, Quebec and wherever prohibited or restricted by law. Subject to all federal, state, local and provincial laws and regulations. For a list of major prize winners (available after 1/29/95): send a self-addressed, stamped envelope entirely separate from your entry to: Sweepstakes Winners, P.O. Box 517, Gibbstown, NJ 08027. Requests must be received by 12/30/94. DO NOT SEND ANY OTHER CORRESPONDENCE TO THIS P.O. BOX.

Bestselling Women's Fiction

Sandra Brown

_____	28951-9 TEXAS! LUCKY	$5.99/6.99 in Canada
_____	28990-X TEXAS! CHASE	$5.99/6.99
_____	29500-4 TEXAS! SAGE	$5.99/6.99
_____	29085-1 22 INDIGO PLACE	$5.99/6.99
_____	29783-X A WHOLE NEW LIGHT	$5.99/6.99
_____	56045-X TEMPERATURES RISING	$5.99/6.99
_____	56274-6 FANTA C	$4.99/5.99
_____	56278-9 LONG TIME COMING	$4.99/5.99

Amanda Quick

_____	28354-5 SEDUCTION	$5.99/6.99
_____	28932-2 SCANDAL	$5.99/6.99
_____	28594-7 SURRENDER	$5.99/6.99
_____	29325-7 RENDEZVOUS	$5.99/6.99
_____	29316-8 RECKLESS	$5.99/6.99
_____	29316-8 RAVISHED	$4.99/5.99
_____	29317-6 DANGEROUS	$5.99/6.99
_____	56506-0 DECEPTION	$5.99/7.50

Nora Roberts

_____	29078-9 GENUINE LIES	$5.99/6.99
_____	28578-5 PUBLIC SECRETS	$5.99/6.99
_____	26461-3 HOT ICE	$5.99/6.99
_____	26574-1 SACRED SINS	$5.99/6.99
_____	27859-2 SWEET REVENGE	$5.99/6.99
_____	27283-7 BRAZEN VIRTUE	$5.99/6.99
_____	29597-7 CARNAL INNOCENCE	$5.50/6.50
_____	29490-3 DIVINE EVIL	$5.99/6.99

Iris Johansen

_____	29871-2 LAST BRIDGE HOME	$4.50/5.50
_____	29604-3 THE GOLDEN BARBARIAN	$4.99/5.99
_____	29244-7 REAP THE WIND	$4.99/5.99
_____	29032-0 STORM WINDS	$4.99/5.99
_____	28855-5 THE WIND DANCER	$4.95/5.95
_____	29968-9 THE TIGER PRINCE	$5.50/6.50
_____	29944-1 THE MAGNIFICENT ROGUE	$5.99/6.99
_____	29945-X BELOVED SCOUNDREL	$5.99/6.99

Ask for these titles at your bookstore or use this page to order.

Please send me the books I have checked above. I am enclosing $ _____ (add $2.50 to cover postage and handling). Send check or money order, no cash or C. O. D.'s please.

Mr./ Ms. _____

Address _____

City/ State/ Zip _____

Send order to: Bantam Books, Dept. FN 16, 2451 S. Wolf Road, Des Plaines, IL 60018
Please allow four to six weeks for delivery.

Prices and availability subject to change without notice.   FN 16 - 4/94